A SUMMER IN OCEAN CITY

CLAUDIA VANCE

CHAPTER ONE

The smell of salt water wafted through Lauren's open car windows as the wind whipped her hair furiously and the bright hot sun poured through the sunroof. As she drove her car over the Ninth Street Bridge into Ocean City, New Jersey, ahead in the distance was the Ferris wheel she'd ridden at least a hundred times as a kid, and on either side of her was the bay, full of boaters and jet skiers enjoying the gorgeous summer day.

"Good to see you again, old friends," Lauren said while smiling at the seagulls, some perched atop the railings and others effortlessly gliding beside her car in the breeze.

The bridge was full of cars packed to the brim with luggage and families. The kids in the car in front of her turned around in the back seat to face her and wave.

Lauren waved back and smiled. "I hope you enjoy your vacation! I know I loved it as a kid down here," she said out loud, though nobody could hear.

By the time she reached the bottom of the bridge and the island, nostalgia came rushing back to her with all the sights and smells. The scent of freshly baked pizza dough, piping-hot doughnuts, and a mix of sunblock and sandy saltwater beaches filled the car. On one corner, people were eating melting ice cream cones while waiting to cross the street, and up ahead on a balcony were beach towels lying over the railings to dry. By now, her hair was a knotty mess from the wind, but it was well worth it to experience this.

Lauren's phone rang, and she quickly answered it as she navigated the streets.

"Are you here?" Nancy, Lauren's mom, asked.

"I literally just got onto the island. It's bumper-to-bumper out here," Lauren said while turning left onto Asbury Avenue.

Nancy laughed. "It's Memorial Day weekend in Ocean City. What did you expect?"

Lauren shrugged. "I don't know. I guess it's been a while since I've been down here. I'm used to the beaches up north."

"Beaches up north?" Nancy asked, confused.

Lauren paused. "Well, yeah. The sandy area near Lake Champlain. I guess that was our 'beach' all these years while living in Vermont."

Nancy chuckled. "You really didn't get to the 'real' beach all of these years?"

Lauren rolled her eyes. "We flew to Mexico and Aruba plenty of times. I'm sure you remember. We got to the beach. We just never had one close by in Vermont."

"Well... welcome back to the Jersey Shore, daughter. I think you're going to enjoy your summer here," Nancy said as she glanced out the window at all of the people walking down the sidewalk in front of her house, carrying beach chairs and coolers. "You sure you don't want to just stay here with us? We have three extra bedrooms, for Pete's sake."

Lauren shook her head as she continued down Asbury Avenue. "Mom, I'm forty-three years old. I need my own place... for my sanity."

Nancy sighed. "Fine, do what you want—"

Lauren cut in. "Is Dad around?"

Nancy shook her head. "Of course not. He's..."

"At the restaurant," they both said in unison.

Nancy paused for a moment. "You know, you didn't have to come to Ocean City to work at the restaurant."

"I know." Lauren came to a stop sign and went into a daze.

A car beeped behind her, startling her out of her thoughts.

"I just want to help," Lauren said as she drove. "You're both retired. You two moved to Ocean City for retirement. You shouldn't be worrying about this restaurant. Dad should be sitting on the beach with you every day, reading the paper and listening to the Phillies' games while eating that huge Italian hoagie he always gets… and you should be reading your books with your big sun hat, sipping your seltzers and lathering on that suntan oil you insist on using that does nothing to protect you."

Nancy laughed. "Oh, that's what you think we should be doing during retirement?"

Lauren shrugged. "I don't know… something along those lines. Okay, I think I'm on my street. I'll call you after I get settled in."

They said their goodbyes, and Lauren pulled up to a large older house by the bay. It was white sided, with tattered blue awnings over the windows and the worst landscaping seen on the island, dead yellow grass patches with one tiny half-alive boxwood bush next to the steps. The house stuck out like a sore thumb among the gorgeous, well-maintained homes in the Gardens neighborhood.

"Well, this is the address. I guess this is my place for the next few months," Lauren said. She suddenly started to regret not staying with her parents as she eyed the ancient-looking window air-conditioning units dangling out of the many windows, along with the worn-out recliner sitting on the front porch.

She popped the trunk and pulled out some of her luggage then carried it up the creaky wooden steps until she was on the front porch, which was even more *interesting* up close. Broken wind chimes dangled in the breeze, trying to make beautiful sounds, but they came off as clunky. About twenty cracked and broken terra cotta pots were piled up in a corner with soil strewn about, and what smelled like rotting fish was coming from somewhere near the side of the house.

Lauren gulped hard as she searched under the torn-up front doormat. She found the key, opened the screen door full of holes, then finally opened the front door.

"Home at last," Lauren said as she opened her eyes, fearing what else she might see.

The house was dark inside, and a musty stench came running from the back of the huge house and smacked her straight in the face, almost knocking her over.

"Ugh. You've got to be kidding me," Lauren said as she carefully placed her luggage inside the door on the worn-out and faded green 1960s carpet.

A small pink love seat with yellow stains sat in the living room. On either side of it were white wicker patio chairs with pink cushions. A tiny black-and-white television sat on a wicker pot stand serving as a makeshift TV stand. Every window had a white shade pulled down, blocking out all light, and was covered by pink lace curtains.

Lauren immediately pulled the shades all the way up in the living room. Then she opened the windows in the room one by one to air the place out.

"Well, at least it has good light," Lauren said as she watched the house slowly perk up with all the sunlight. "This isn't so bad. It really isn't," she said to console herself. Maybe if she said it, she'd believe it.

"Okay, time to check out the kitchen." She walked into a tiny pink kitchen. It had chipped black-and-white tiles on the floor and old faux-wood Formica countertops.

Lauren opened the oven and found a huge mouse nest inside. She slammed the oven door shut and screamed so loud that houses blocks away could have heard. "Oh, no. No. No. No!" she said while running for her luggage. She quickly scooped it up and ran out the front door, locking it behind her, and to her car, where she threw the luggage into the back seat. She hopped in the front and immediately turned the car on while putting on her seat belt. She put the car in reverse, ready to peel out of the driveway, but a knock on her passenger car window stopped her.

"Hi!" a woman walking a dachshund said with a smile.

Lauren rolled down her passenger-side window. "Oh, hello. I was just..."

"Leaving?" the woman asked while chuckling.

Lauren felt the tension leave her body as she started laughing at the absurdity of the situation. "Yes. I rented this place, and it's not at all what the pictures showed in the listing."

"I'm Erin," the woman said while waving. "If you stay, I'll be your next-door neighbor. Well, we'll be, my husband and I. Anyway, are you sure you have the right address? Nobody has stayed at this place in years. It's been vacant."

Lauren pulled up the rental listing on her phone and showed Erin. "Yup. Here's the listing."

Erin shook her head in disbelief. "Mind if I take this and look at it? I'm just shocked they're renting this out without any kind of work being done to it first."

"Go right ahead," Lauren said, feeling justified for her disappointment.

Erin scrolled through the photos with widened eyes. "These pictures are at least ten years old, back when it was somewhat kept up. I'm so sorry this happened to you," she said, handing the phone back. "Maybe you can call and complain and find another rental."

Lauren shook her head. "There aren't any others in my budget. I got this last minute a couple weeks ago, and now I see why."

Erin frowned. "I'm so sorry. Truly. Maybe you can make it work somehow?"

Lauren sighed as she looked back at the tattered screen door. "I don't know about that. Well, it was lovely meeting you, Erin."

"Good luck," Erin said as she waved goodbye.

Lauren took off down the street in her car.

* * *

"Well, I guess I was right," Nancy said as she stood in the doorway of one of her guest bedrooms and Lauren unzipped her suitcase on the bed. "You should have just planned on staying here all along."

Lauren sighed as she walked out toward the living room, her mother following behind. "It's just for a night or two until I figure out if I can get a refund for this house I rented."

"You better get a refund. A mouse nest in the oven? That's disgusting! I wouldn't stay there for free!" Nancy yelled over the Phillies game blaring loudly from the living room, where Joe, Lauren's father, sat with his feet kicked up after a long morning at the restaurant.

"Your mother's right. We've got a perfectly fine bedroom for you here. Only two blocks to the beach, too," Joe said, pointing out the window.

Lauren paused to compose herself. "Look, it's not that I don't love you two and want to stay here, but having my own place for the next few months is important to me. If I were here for a week, that'd be one thing," she said as she took her phone and called Jen, the Realtor she had used, while stepping out the back door into the yard.

"Hello. Sunshine and Sand Realtors," said the voice on the other end.

Lauren tensed up, not sure of how to handle the situation.

"Hi. I'm looking for Jen. I rented a house on 5532 Bay Road, and—"

"Oh, that was you? Oh, okay. Well, this is Jen," the woman said as she typed on her computer.

Lauren shifted her eyes, not sure of what that meant. "Yes, that was me… unfortunately. Anyway, the place has so many issues with it that I don't know where to begin. I want a refund and possibly a new place."

Jen paused and sighed. "I knew this was going to happen. I knew it. I told the owner to not list the place for rent, but he insisted. The owner is in his eighties, family inheritance. He didn't want the house. It became his about five years ago when a friend left it to him in their will. Well, now he's in a retirement community and can't be bothered with it. No children, no wife, and he has this house here still. Are you interested in buying it? I'm sure I can work something out."

"What? Buying it? Are you crazy?" Lauren asked, astonished.

Jen shrugged. "The house may be run-down, but it's prime real estate. Right on the bay, great neighborhood."

Lauren shook her head. "I'm only here for the summer to help my family's business. Then it's back to Vermont for me, thankfully."

Jen bit her lip. "Look, Fred is the name of the man who owns this house. I like him. Good man. I think he's counting on this money to help him get settled in his new place. I can ask him if we can knock off five hundred dollars a month for this hassle, but honestly… I don't know anywhere on the island you're going to find a place to rent for two thousand dollars a month. It's unheard of here in the summer. Even two thousand dollars a week is pretty rare."

Lauren rolled her eyes. "Yeah, unless it's a dump."

"Well, how about this? Stay there for a few nights. Clean it to your specifications. Rearrange some things. See how you like it. See if it's doable for you, and if it's not, get back to me, and we'll work something out, okay?" Jen asked.

Lauren sighed deeply as she looked around her parents' well-manicured lawn and shrubs. "Okay, I can do that, but I'm not making any promises."

Nancy came outside through the back door just as Lauren ended the call. "Well... what did they say?"

"My Realtor, Jen, wants me to basically clean the house to my standards and spend a few nights there before making my decision," Lauren said as she popped a mint into her mouth.

"Is she serious?" Nancy asked, shocked. "There was a mouse nest in the oven."

Lauren rolled her eyes. "Well, it looks like I've got my work cut out for me."

Joe opened the back door, letting the loud Phillies game spill outside with him. "What are we doing for dinner tonight, hon?"

Nancy, feeling frustrated, shrugged. "Joe, I don't know. What do you want?"

"I could go for some crab cakes," Joe said as the Phillies' announcer yelled about a double play. He immediately ran back to the television to see what he'd missed.

"Look, you just drove seven hours. Stay the night here in a nice, cool bedroom without rats in the oven, have dinner with us, and tomorrow, I'll help you tackle this... dump. Does that sound like a plan?" Nancy asked matter-of-factly.

Lauren nodded. "Sounds great, and you don't have to help me clean. You two have enough on your plate, trying to keep the restaurant afloat."

Nancy shook her head. "Don't even get me started on the restaurant. We'll talk about that after you're settled. There's a lot to discuss," Nancy said as she headed back inside.

Lauren stood alone outside with just the sounds of the ocean in the background and a sinking feeling in her gut. She wondered why she'd uprooted her life for this and if she'd made the wrong decision by coming back to Ocean City. Suddenly, she was homesick for Vermont... and her old life with Steven.

CHAPTER TWO

The next morning, Lauren hesitantly walked up the steps to her summer rental. For being Memorial Day weekend, it was pretty quiet out except for some seagulls passing above. Then again, maybe everyone on the island hadn't woken up yet since it was seven a.m. She wasn't normally one to get up early, but she couldn't sleep more than a few hours in her parent's guest room the night before. She'd woken up at five a.m. and spent the next hour or so staring up at the whizzing ceiling fan as her mind filled with thoughts. She still couldn't believe that she'd left her life in Vermont to be in Ocean City for the next few months. It didn't feel real.

As she approached the front door, she crinkled her nose, noticing the fishy smell still lingering on the porch, then she spotted some animal's paw prints throughout the spilled potting soil. *Raccoons*, she thought to herself.

Lauren gulped hard as she turned the key in the front door lock, afraid of what she might find this time around.

Once the door opened, Lauren stepped inside to the musty smell but tried to ignore it. She was there to take a proper tour of the house. If she wanted her own space for the summer, this rental was going to have to work somehow.

She walked quickly through the foyer to the kitchen again, only glancing at the oven, and headed straight to the cabinets. The first cabinet had five plastic to-go containers. The second cabinet held just a used yellow dish sponge. Then she flipped a third cabinet open to reveal a mason jar full of nails and screws.

Lauren shook her head and closed the cabinet. "I guess pots, pans, and dishes are a thing of the past for summer houses these days," she said sarcastically. She then pulled out a drawer to find loose rusted silverware piled inside as though it was a junk drawer that people just threw things into without any thought.

"How is this acceptable?" Lauren blurted out, growing frustrated.

She took a deep breath and composed herself then headed to the small dining room adjacent to the kitchen. It was dark, so she flicked on the light switch. The lone lightbulb in the chandelier turned on then popped off. Lauren rolled her eyes and immediately walked to the windows, where she opened the curtains and pulled up the shades, and the sunlight allowed her to see the room. A card table sat in the middle with old mismatched wooden chairs all around it.

Lauren put her hands on her face, feeling overwhelmed, but then saw, in the corner of the dining room, a beautiful upright piano. She slowly pulled out the stool and sat at the piano, happiness rising up through her chest. She'd taken piano lessons for most of her childhood, and years had passed since she touched a piano. She cracked her knuckles and played a few notes, then a noise in the backyard caught her attention. She got up to look out the window, but it was blocked by a huge overgrown shrub, so she walked back through the kitchen and through the laundry room to the back door and opened it with a jolt.

"Unreal," Lauren said as the fresh air poured onto her through the doorway.

Her eyes sparkled in the sunlight as she stepped out onto a large stained deck off the back of the house. She walked toward the railing to see the big beautiful blue bay before her. It was, in one word, magnificent. Whoever had been maintaining the home seemed to have only put any effort into the deck and not much else, for it was in pristine condition. Lauren closed her eyes and took a deep breath then opened them again to see a couple of boats passing by. Then she noticed, among the high grass of the very overgrown yard, steps leading down from the deck to a private dock. Vines and weeds had grown all over it, but it was just waiting for someone to use it. Suddenly, voices could be heard from the front of the house.

"Lauren! You in here?"

Lauren cocked her head in confusion, not expecting anyone at that time of day. "I'm out back!" she yelled, still not sure whom she was talking to.

Just then, two black Labradors came stampeding toward her with leashes dragging behind. They wiggled their butts as Lauren scratched their heads.

"Claire?" Lauren called out, bewildered.

Claire, Lauren's older sister, laughed as her kids, Evan and Bridget, aged nine and eleven, ran toward Lauren with arms wide open for hugs from their aunt. "We just got here. Mom told us where you were, so we thought we'd stop here first to see the new digs," Claire said as she walked out onto the deck with wide eyes, seemingly overcome by the view. "Wow, look at *this*. This is incredible."

Lauren hugged Claire and the kids. "This is a surprise! I thought you weren't getting in until next week."

Claire sighed. "I was going to wait for Brian to be done in the office next week, to come down, but he told us to head here without him, and you know with my job, I can work anywhere. He'll be down next week. The kids just finished their school year. So, here we are, ready to tackle the summer Jersey style."

Lauren looked at her watch. "It's seven thirty a.m. You left

Pennsylvania at four thirty in the morning to get here? Are you crazy?" she asked, laughing.

Claire shrugged. "I wanted to beat traffic. Everyone is headed to New Jersey beaches for the weekend. I didn't want to be stuck in that mess. Plus, the kids just slept in the car the whole way," she said as she looked back toward the house. "Feel like giving us a tour?"

Lauren smiled. "You came at a good time. I'm still taking a proper tour. Aside from the deck, this house is *awful*. It apparently has been owned by Fred, an older gentleman who inherited it and never kept up with it. Not sure who owned it before him. Anyway, the Realtor I used basically told me that it's this house or nothing at this point."

Claire nodded. "I did notice the smell when I walked in. It reminded me of some of those older summer houses our parents rented when we were kids. Almost like the scent of wood paneling mixed with cigarette-stenched carpets."

"Mixed with must," Lauren chimed in. "Glad I'm not the only one noticing this. Let's start with the upstairs since I haven't seen it yet," she said as she led the way.

They all walked up the creaky green-carpeted steps till they reached the top.

"How many bedrooms is it?" Claire asked as she peered down the hallway full of closed doors.

"I think it said three?" Lauren said as she opened the first door to their right.

Just like the rest of the house, the room was dark.

Claire flicked the light switch on and gasped as Lauren opened the curtains. "What is *that*?" Claire asked, pointing at the corner.

Evan covered his eyes and ran from the room, while Lauren, Claire, and Bridget stared in disbelief.

"Clowns?" Bridget asked as she walked toward a seven-foot bookshelf full of every type of clown trinket and doll one could think of.

Lauren shook her head. "Oh, we're *not* doing this. I'm not staying in a house with creepy clowns."

Claire laughed. "Did Fred collect clowns?"

Lauren shrugged. "You know as much as I do at this point. Well, this will *not* be my bedroom—that's for sure," she said as she turned off the lights. Then she quickly ushered everyone out of the room and closed the door.

"And what's behind door number two?" Claire asked jokingly as she put a hand on the next doorknob and looked back at everyone hesitantly.

"Hopefully, not more clowns," Evan said as a shiver went down his spine.

Claire swung the door open, and they stood there stunned as their eyes scanned the huge four-poster bed complete with a canopy. A gorgeous vintage dresser had dried hydrangeas on top, and green velvet drapes over the windows just grazed the floor.

"Would you look at this?" Lauren said as she walked around, admiring the room.

"It feels like it's straight out of an old movie. Maybe *Gone with the Wind*," Claire said as she ran a finger through the thick dust on the dresser.

Bridget hoisted herself up onto the bed and plopped down hard, causing a plume of dust to appear.

"Bridget, get off there. You're going to be covered in dust," Claire said as she waved her hands in front of her face.

Lauren sighed as she walked out of the bedroom. "It would have been nice if they had hired a cleaner to come before I got here."

Claire shook her head in disgust. "Call the Realtor, and have them send someone out. This is not acceptable."

Lauren laughed. "Wait until you see the kitchen. Not a dish or pot to be found. Oh, and don't get me started on the mouse nest in the oven. Also, the living room—"

Claire cut in. "Excuse me. Did you say a mouse nest in the oven?" she asked, a horrified look on her face.

Lauren walked to the third closed door and opened it while looking back at Claire. "Yup."

"Look, just stay at Mom and Dad's with us. This is insane. You shouldn't be staying here," Claire said. "They have three guest rooms. The kids can share a room. You can have the third."

Lauren paused in thought as she stared into the third bedroom. It had a queen bed with a blue-and-white quilt and multiple pillows on top. It appeared to be the only room in the house that already had the shade up and curtains drawn.

Claire walked over to the dresser in the corner and ran a finger over the top. "That's weird. No dust," she said, staring at her finger.

"It's odd. It's like this is the only room that someone was living in," Lauren said, noticing that not a speck of dust or dirt could be seen anywhere, unlike the previous rooms.

"Here's the bathroom!" Evan and Bridget yelled from the hallway.

Lauren and Claire rushed out to see it, stopping in their tracks when they saw that it looked completely remodeled and modern.

"Nothing makes sense in this house." Lauren laughed, trying to find the humor of it all. "The deck and the bathroom took priority over everything."

Claire laughed. "I'll say. I still think you should stay at Mom and Dad's with us. It'll be fun. Like old times," she said as she led the way back downstairs with everyone in tow.

Lauren walked into the living room and plopped onto the wicker chair, dangling her legs off the armrest. "I don't know. It's just important for me to live on my own during this time. You know?"

Claire nodded. "I get it. You have to find yourself after the divorce."

Lauren sighed. "Plus, I'm going to be seeing you guys all of the time anyway." She pointed at the small black-and-white TV on the plant stand. "Did you see my fancy television?"

Bridget and Evan walked over to the tiny television with an antenna and studied it like they were seeing something from their history books for the first time. The fact was they probably were.

"*This* is a TV?" Evan asked, shocked.

Lauren nodded and chuckled. "Yes, and there isn't a remote. You have to get up and turn this dial on the front to get to a channel."

"What's the point?" Bridget asked.

Claire and Lauren laughed as the dogs came barreling down the steps, apparently spooked by something.

"I think they saw the clowns," Evan said, causing everyone to burst out laughing.

Claire sighed as she looked around the house. "I'll help clean. The kids can go hang on the beach with Mom and Dad."

"You sure?" Lauren asked. "Do you really want to spend part of your Memorial Day weekend cleaning?"

Claire rolled her eyes. "No, not really… but I know this is important to you, and I think if we add music and some open windows with bay air, we could have some fun doing it. I only ask that you let me come over and sit on the deck whenever I please."

"Deal," Lauren said as her phone started ringing.

"Hello?" she answered.

"Lauren? It's Jen, your Realtor over at Sunshine and Sand Realtors.

"Oh, hi…" Lauren said and mouthed to Claire that it was the Realtor.

"Ask her to send a cleaner over at the owner's expense," Claire mouthed back.

"Look, I spoke with Fred, the owner, and he's willing to

give you back five hundred dollars to use toward cleaning and any other items you may need," Jen said as she swallowed hard. "Also, I didn't realize it hadn't been formally cleaned. I think there was some miscommunication there. I tried to call a cleaning service, but they're all booked up, some companies even months in advance. Will five hundred cut it for you?"

Lauren took a deep breath, suddenly feeling sorry for Fred having to deal with this inherited mess all while transitioning to a retirement home. She glanced at Claire, who was staring at her, waiting to hear what they were talking about. "That should work. My sister is here, and she's going to help. We'll have to buy dishes, silverware, and some pots. Probably some linens, towels, and lightbulbs. Probably a vacuum and tons of cleaning products. Who knows what else…?"

Jen propped her forehead in her hands. "There aren't dishes or silverware? Are you serious?"

Lauren sighed. "Well, technically there is silverware, but it's all rusted and filthy. I'm not using it."

Jen nodded. "I get it. Look, it sounds like you need more than five hundred dollars. How about I get you eight hundred back. That should cover your time cleaning as well."

"That would be wonderful," Lauren said as she gave Claire a thumbs-up. "I really appreciate you doing this for me."

"Glad I can help. Text me your email, and after I speak to Fred, I'll Venmo you the money. Talk soon," Jen said as she hung up.

"Well, that went well," Lauren said, feeling somewhat relieved.

"Great. They're sending over a cleaning service?" Claire asked.

Lauren shook her head. "No, the cleaning companies are all booked up around here. They're getting me eight hundred dollars to buy cleaning supplies and everything else I need. We're all set to start this big ol' project."

Claire shifted her eyes. "Great. Can't wait."

"That's what big sisters are for. How about we fuel up on some takeout breakfast after we drop the dogs off with Mom and Dad?" Lauren asked as she put an arm around Claire's shoulders and headed toward the front door.

Lauren and Claire made their way back onto the front porch while Evan and Bridget went ahead of them to take the dogs to the front yard. Lauren stopped in her tracks just as the neighbor next door pulled up in a Jeep Wrangler, hauling some surfboards in the back. He got out in a partially unzipped wet suit and ran his fingers through his thick golden-brown hair before pulling one of the surfboards out the back window.

"Who's *that*?" Claire asked.

Lauren stared in awe. "I'm not sure... but he looks like he's doing a Calvin Klein model shoot. Look at those forearm muscles."

The man walked behind the Wrangler, holding his surfboard, when he noticed them staring from the porch. He smiled and nodded. "Hey there!"

Lauren froze and sank down into a squat, pretending not to hear him. Meanwhile, Claire waved both her hands in the air. "Hi! A beautiful day for modeling... I mean surfing!"

Lauren covered her face with her hands. "Claire, you did not just say *modeling*."

Claire laughed. "Well, at least I'm talking to him and not hiding. What are you doing down there *anyway*?"

Lauren quickly searched around and found a quarter. "This. I dropped this," she said while standing up.

Claire shifted her eyes. "Right. Well, you should be the one chatting with this guy. He's your neighbor, not mine. Plus, I'm happily married."

Lauren watched as the neighbor walked around to the back of his house. "Well, I guess there's always next time. It's weird. There was something so familiar about him. It caught me off guard."

Claire laughed. "I'll say. I've never seen you act that a way around a man before. You're always so cool and collected."

Lauren shrugged. "You're used to seeing me with Steven. I was comfortable around him."

Claire shook her head. "Nope, even before Steven, you always had this confidence about you when it came to meeting new people. I always admired that about you."

Lauren sighed. "Thanks, sis. At this point, I think I've forgotten who I used to be."

CHAPTER THREE

"So much for takeout," Lauren said while cutting into her golden blueberry waffle at Uncle Bill's Restaurant on Twenty-First and Asbury.

Claire shrugged. "I've been thinking about having breakfast at Uncle Bill's for months now. I needed their pancakes." she said, pouring syrup over them. "Plus, we just shopped until we dropped after I drove for three hours. I am famished."

Lauren nodded as she took a bite. "I'm surprised the kids didn't want to come get something to eat."

"Me, too, but Mom offered to take them to the beach, and they'll never turn down a chance to swim in the ocean. She brought a bunch of food for them. They're set." Claire savored the buttery, sweet flavor of her pancakes.

Lauren nodded and sighed. "I have a feeling we're going to be cleaning for hours."

Claire took that as her cue and nodded at the waitress walking by with a hot pot of coffee, who then refilled her cup.

Lauren finished her waffle and dabbed her mouth with her napkin. "Do you think I got everything I need?"

Claire sipped her coffee. "We filled the entire back of my

minivan. You're good," she said then took her last bite of breakfast.

Lauren laughed. "It really felt like I was shopping for my college dorm all over again. Bath mats, sheets, towels…"

"It did, didn't it? Made me a little nostalgic too," Claire said with a sigh. "Being here again with you makes me nostalgic. How have you not visited Ocean City all these years? Not even to stop by the restaurant?"

Lauren shrugged. "I don't know. I guess I just got so consumed with my life in Vermont. Plus, Grandma and Grandpa only opened the restaurant in the summer, which is when I was super busy with work. Mom and Dad only came here sporadically, and it seems all my high school friends moved to other parts of the country, so it's not like I could meet up with them at the beach, really. Plus, you and Brian and the kids were going exclusively to Delaware beaches for a while."

Claire nodded. "That's where Brian's family had been going for years. I kind of got sucked into that tradition. Luckily, that all changed this year since Mom and Dad moved down here after retirement. Now, it's time for *my* family's traditions."

"I kind of like that," Lauren said with a smile.

Claire finished her coffee and stood up. "You about ready to head back over to the house and get started?"

"Let's do it. Breakfast is on me," Lauren said as she hurried to the register with the check before Claire could try to beat her to it.

* * *

Lauren plugged in the new vacuum and got to work on the carpet in the living room, noticing a ton of stuff was getting sucked up. "Wow. It's looking so much better already!" Lauren yelled over the noise.

Claire had on rubber dish gloves up to her elbows as she

21

squatted in front of the oven, taking deep breaths. "I can do this. Doing it for my sister… Because I love her!" she yelled back.

"What?" Lauren asked.

"I'm tackling the mouse nest for you," Claire said as she opened the oven.

Lauren turned off the vacuum and walked into the kitchen. "You don't have to do that… Really, Claire."

Claire reached into the oven and pulled out tons of fluffy white stuff, throwing it into a garbage bag. "Well, I'm doing it and getting it over with. This is so gnarly. Where do they even find this material?"

Lauren shrugged. "Beats me. Does it look vacated? No mice to be found?"

Claire took out the remaining nesting material. "All good. I'll get to work cleaning and sanitizing it next."

"You're the best," Lauren said as she headed back toward the vacuum in the living room.

* * *

Nine hours later, Lauren shoved a quilt and sheets into the washer and pulled another set of sheets and a duvet out of the dryer. She folded them neatly into a laundry basket and brought them upstairs to Claire, who was on her hands and knees, scrubbing the bathroom tiles.

Lauren dropped the basket on the floor and sighed. "I think we've got enough done that I feel comfortable being here now. Thank you so much, Claire."

Claire stood up and pulled off her dish gloves and threw them into the bathroom trash can then leaned against the doorframe. "We mopped everything, vacuumed, dusted, cleaned all surfaces, disinfected, cleaned out the cabinets, and stuck the new dishes, glasses, and everything else in them.

What am I missing? Oh yeah, washed the bedding and swept the front porch."

Lauren laughed. "The clowns are all put away in a box, and we even got that nasty, stinky recliner off the porch. I guess that's where that rotting-fish smell was coming from. There's a reason inside furniture is not meant to be outside. I don't think the owner will care that it's now on the curb for trash pickup."

"Oh, definitely not," Claire said as she looked out the bathroom window to see the sun had set and it was dark outside. "What time is it?"

"Nine thirty," Lauren said with disbelief. "I can't believe how much we've gotten done. I'm utterly exhausted. Let's call it a day. We did everything that needs to be done. I just have to tackle the yard at some point, but that's not important," Lauren said as she yawned.

Claire yawned as well and gave Lauren a hug. "Okay, well, call me if you need anything. I guess I'll head out," she said as she pulled out her phone to see that Brian was calling her.

"Hey, hon," Claire said as she answered the phone while heading back downstairs.

"Thanks again, Claire! Also, lock the door behind you!" Lauren yelled.

"You're welcome, and will do," Claire replied as Lauren listened for the dead bolt click.

Lauren made the bed with the newly washed bedding then hopped into the shower, washing off all the grime and dirt. Nothing felt better in that moment than that shower, and afterward, her soft pajamas felt like heaven.

She was too tired to even think, so she turned on her bedside lamp and got into bed. She had chosen the room with the four-poster bed. After it was fully cleaned and dusted, it just felt so luxurious, compared to the other rooms, like staying in a fancy bedroom at an old bed-and-breakfast. Her luggage was unpacked into the dresser and her summer reading books stacked on the bedside table. She even sprayed the room with a lavender mist and cracked the windows for an evening breeze. Already, it felt cozy. She pulled the fresh sheets over herself, fluffed her pillows one last time, turned off the lamp, and immediately fell asleep.

After a few hours, a strange noise abruptly woke her. *Bang!*

Lauren sat straight up with her heart racing, waiting quietly to hear the noise again.

Click. Click. Creak.

Lauren widened her eyes, still sitting in the dark, trying to make sense of the noise.

Slam! A door had been slammed shut in the house.

Lauren immediately turned on the bedside lamp and got up and locked her bedroom door while texting Claire.

Did you lock the front door before you left? she hurriedly typed.

A few moments passed, and she got a text back.

"Yes. Now can I go back to sleep please?"

Lauren felt like her heart was going to beat out of her chest. *Claire, someone slammed a door in this house while I was sleeping. I'm going to freak out.*

Lauren waited for a response, but Claire had apparently turned her phone to silent and fallen back to sleep. She couldn't blame her. Their day and evening had been utterly tiring. They had managed to scarf down some sandwiches in ten minutes around five thirty, but they'd cleaned the rest of the time.

As she stood by the bedroom door, hand shaking, she unlocked it then slowly opened it, peering into the dark hallway. "This feels like something out of a horror movie," Lauren muttered as she cautiously made her way downstairs, starting to feel sick to her stomach.

Then, there it was again. *Bang!*

Lauren screamed and jumped as she felt every hair on her body stand on edge. She turned around and saw the back door had never been fully shut and was now swinging back and forth due to the air circulation from the opened windows.

Lauren immediately shut and locked the back door then closed all the windows. She flopped onto the pink love seat in the living room and turned the lamp on, staring around the quiet but creaky house, eyeing everything around her, almost as if she was warning the house to not try that nonsense again. An old clock on the wall could be heard ticking, then the refrigerator started humming.

Lauren sighed as she propped her head on one hand. "Well, I'm wide awake now at... midnight," she said to nobody while glancing at her phone. She got up and turned on the little black-and-white TV, then moved the dial from station to station, but an infomercial for a raincoat that turned into an umbrella was the only interesting thing on. With that, she turned off the TV, put on her light hoodie, and slipped her shoes on. Then she headed out the front door with her keys and phone.

The night was warm and calm outside, much different from Lauren's expectations, with the slamming back door. Perhaps the wind had died down already. The air smelled of murky bay water, and the majority of the neighbors appeared to be in for the evening as everything felt mostly quiet. She made a left at the sidewalk and started walking around her neighborhood, something she hadn't had a second to do yet.

She smiled as she looked at all the beautiful homes. The first house she walked by didn't look like a seasonal home like Lauren's. The landscaping was far too intricate, and she could see framed family photos on the wall when she glanced in. *I think this is where Erin lives*, Lauren thought. That was the neighbor she'd run into when she first got to her rental. She approached the second house and peered up to see a gentleman running on a treadmill in the upstairs window. "Gotta get that exercise in when you can." Lauren chuckled to herself. Then the third house was a smaller blue cottage with a front porch where a teenager and his girlfriend appeared to be watching a movie projected on a white sheet tacked up by its corners, above the railing. Lauren smiled as she passed, noticing they were cuddled up together, watching *American Pie*, probably at the start of their summer romance. She remembered that feeling all too well. There was a certain magic to being young and in love, especially in the summer when the nights were warm and life just felt simpler and happier.

Lauren's mind began wandering, suddenly wondering what Steven was doing. She stopped herself. She didn't need to be thinking of him, not after everything that had happened. She continued walking around the neighborhood, noticing the smell of fabric softener wafting from a dryer vent and the sounds of crickets chirping and frogs croaking. The crescent moon was shining bright above, and while she might not have loved her rental house, she surely was falling in love with the neighborhood. She made her way around the sidewalks for another twenty minutes before making a full circle and approaching her Calvin Klein–model neighbor's house, which was to the right of her house. The curtains on all his windows were open, and she couldn't help but slow down and look. She noticed the soft glow of a lamp in a sunroom on the side of the house and the profile of a man sitting in a chair, looking down at a book.

He likes to read, Lauren thought, feeling a growing curiosity. She glanced over at his porch, noticing he had a variety of house plants situated beautifully around it, some spider plants hanging from macrame hangers and succulents clustered together on small wooden end tables. She stopped dead in her tracks when she noticed a woman with short hair walking through the house and toward the neighbor reading. Lauren watched as she stood before him and leaned down to kiss him. He barely looked up from his book when they kissed, though.

What was that about? Lauren thought as she started to walk again, not noticing a huge branch in front of her. She stepped on it, causing the loudest snap possible. She felt like it echoed off every house in the neighborhood. Not knowing what to do, she glanced back in the window, and the neighbor had put down his book and was staring straight at her. The woman wasn't in the room anymore, and time seemed to stand still as Lauren stared back, not sure of who she was really looking at. *Keep your cool. Just play it off as nothing,* Lauren thought as she continued walking. She got to her front door, let herself in, and immediately ran upstairs back into the bedroom, feeling her heart race again, this time over the weird run-in with her neighbor—not a great way to start off the summer in the new house.

She heard a text come through and looked at her phone.

"Someone slammed a door in your house? Who?" Claire had written back.

Lauren laughed, knowing her sister had probably woken up to go to the bathroom and checked her phone in the process.

"The back door was open, and the breeze was making it slam. All good over here. I don't have any ghosts or intruders as initially suspected," Lauren texted back.

Claire never wrote back, probably having fallen asleep again before finding out if a stranger was walking around, slamming doors in her sister's house.

Before getting back in bed, Lauren crouched down to discreetly peer out her window. She looked to the left at Erin's house. The lights appeared to be turned off. Then she gazed to the right at her other neighbor's, but this time she noticed he was standing on the porch, looking out at the street with his arms crossed in thought. The streetlamp cast a glow on him, and he looked even more handsome.

Lauren sighed as she pulled herself away from the window and got back into bed under the freshly cleaned sheets and duvet. She wanted to be at the restaurant nice and early tomorrow, so she needed to get some shut-eye. She quickly dozed off into a deep slumber, but still with the bedroom door locked just in case.

CHAPTER FOUR

Early the next morning, Lauren sipped her coffee as she walked into Chipper's, her grandparents' restaurant, technically owned by her parents. It had been a long-loved staple in Ocean City for sixty years, and it had some of the best views of the beach and ocean. It was only open for breakfast, and even though it opened at seven a.m., people would start lining up at the door at six thirty to secure their spots. It was cash only, and the restaurant itself had a small old Airstream-diner feel, with the original red booths and a wraparound counter with red swivel stools bolted into the floor. Outside was a little more modern, with some tables and chairs.

"Well, look who it is!" an older gentleman said as Lauren looked around the busy diner.

She furrowed her brow, unsure of who he was.

"You don't remember me, do you?" The man chuckled.

Lauren shook her head while studying his face. "I can't say I do."

The man nodded just as Joe, her dad, put a plate of creamed chipped beef down in front him.

"Lauren, it's Mr. Young. He's been a regular forever. You used to sit next to him at the counter as a little girl while eating your Cheerios," Joe said as he threw a dish towel over his shoulder.

Lauren's jaw dropped as she threw a hand over her mouth in shock. "I can't believe it. It's so good to see you after all these years."

Mr. Young smiled. "It's great to see you all grown up. What are you up to these days?"

Lauren set her purse behind the counter and tied a black apron around her waist. "I'm here for the summer, trying to help my parents figure out how to run this place."

Mr. Young nodded. "Well, your grandparents ran this place like a well-oiled machine for all those years, and then your uncle took over for about ten years. It looks like the buck was passed to your parents now."

Lauren sighed. "Yeah, because Uncle Mike moved to Florida, leaving my poor retired parents to keep this shore treasure afloat."

Mr. Young nodded and took a bite of his breakfast. "That's where you come in."

Before Lauren could say anything, her dad handed her two plates of hot French toast made right on the cooktop behind the counter. That was one of the perks of sitting at the counter, watching the food being cooked.

"Take this over to booth number three, please," her dad said as he rushed to the back.

Lauren paused, realizing she didn't have a clue which booth was number three. She wondered why he couldn't have just said something like "the two women wearing red shirts" or "the couple with the playful baby."

Mr. Young pointed at the booth in the corner. "I've been coming here long enough to know that booth is number three."

Lauren gave a sigh of relief. "Mr. Young, you're the best. I hope you're here a lot. I have a feeling I'm going to need your knowledge more often than not."

Mr. Young laughed and took a bite of his creamed chipped beef. "You're in luck. I'm here all the time."

* * *

By nine a.m., Chipper's was packed inside and outside, including twenty-five people waiting for tables. The cooks were completely backed up with orders, and the cool-and-collected attitude Lauren's dad had at seven a.m. was now frazzled and stressed.

"Can you ring these people up, Lauren?" her dad asked as he whizzed by with a tray of plates.

"I'll be right there after I drop these drinks off outside," Lauren said as she headed out the door.

The people waiting to pay looked around the restaurant, half annoyed they had to wait as Lauren rushed back in.

"Did you enjoy your breakfast?" Lauren asked, out of breath as she rang up their check.

"We did. Are you guys… doing okay here?" the guy asked as he handed her money.

Lauren handed them their change. "We're trying. It's a little new to this side of the family."

"Oh, okay. We just never had to wait that long for our meals to come out, and we noticed the table next to us never got the refills they asked for. Well, I hope you work the kinks out," the man said as he and his wife turned around and exited the restaurant.

Lauren paused in thought and looked around the restaurant, noticing the other servers rushing around but also seeing many empty drinks and customers seating themselves at tables that hadn't been bussed yet. Also, the air conditioning seemed to be having issues as the room was suddenly feeling really hot.

"Lauren, I need your help," her dad said as he stood before her.

Lauren snapped out of her thoughts.

"We only have two cartons of eggs left. I didn't order enough. Go to the grocery store, and buy as many as you can," he said as he placed a credit card in her hand.

"You can handle my tables?" Lauren asked as she picked up her purse.

"Yes. Go. Now!" her dad said as sweat poured from his temples.

Lauren ran out the front doors to her car and hightailed it to the grocery store, which wasn't exactly around the corner. She managed to pick up a ton of eggs and had them back within thirty minutes.

She pulled up to the restaurant and was met by three of the cooks, who looked completely relieved to see her. She popped the trunk, and they immediately hauled all the cartons inside to the kitchen. She then walked back into the restaurant to see her dad looking ready to have a total meltdown.

"Dad, what do you need? I'm back," Lauren said as she put a hand on his shoulder.

"Great. Run this order to the couple outside. I don't even remember what table number it goes to. The ticket flew away somewhere. Maybe ask around," he said as he handed her a tray and rushed back into the kitchen.

Lauren nodded and gulped hard as she went out the door with the food, quickly finding the table it went to, luckily. As she stopped to clear a table the bussers hadn't gotten to yet, she wondered if Uncle Mike had given her parents any inkling of how to run the restaurant, unless her uncle had the same stress they were having. Maybe that was why he'd left the business and moved to Florida so abruptly.

* * *

It was two in the afternoon, the restaurant was cleaned and closed, and Lauren was in her bathing suit, holding a beach bag, chair, and towel on the Fourteenth Street beach. She spotted her sister and, without saying a word, plopped her stuff down and dramatically lay down on Claire's towel under the Ocean City Fishing Club, staring up at the wood planks of the pier above.

"Long first day at the restaurant?" Claire asked as she applied sunblock to her arms.

Lauren didn't take her eyes off the pier. "Longest day of my life. What did I get myself into? What did our parents get themselves into?"

Claire shrugged as she watched Evan and Bridget playing catch with some kids nearby. "I'm scared to ask what happened. I offered to help out tomorrow so Mom doesn't have to go in."

Lauren sat up and hoisted herself into her beach chair. "I don't think our parents know how to run a restaurant."

Claire laughed. "You think? Dad was a superintendent the last twenty years, and Mom worked as a nurse. They know absolutely nothing. I had a feeling this was going to be a mess."

Lauren stared at her sister. "So, is that why you're in Ocean City this summer as well?"

Claire rolled her eyes. "Pretty much. I have the kids, so I won't be able to help out as much as you. However, it gave me a good reason to be here the whole summer when I ran it by Brian. By the way... did you end up being able to sleep last night?"

Lauren laughed. "Actually, yeah. Once I figured out a ghost wasn't slamming doors around the house, I ended up taking a walk around the neighborhood. I think that helped because I went right to sleep afterward. By the way, I saw that guy, my neighbor, in his house, kissing some woman."

Claire widened her eyes. "You were *spying* on him?"

Lauren rolled her eyes and put on her sunglasses while lying back in her chair. "No, I wasn't spying on him. I happened to be walking by and glanced in his windows."

Claire chuckled. "Whatever you say. So, he has a girlfriend. Or maybe wife?"

Lauren shook her head. "Definitely not a wife. He didn't have a ring on the other day."

Claire shifted her eyes. "How did you notice that? You only looked at him for a few seconds before you dropped to the floor."

"I notice things. That's all I'm going to say," Lauren said and looked around the beach, taking note of a man walking with a cooler and selling ice cream and popsicles. "I'm about ready to get some ice cream. I didn't get a second to eat anything today."

Claire waved her hand in the air. "I've got hot dogs wrapped in foil."

Lauren laughed. "Like Mom used to do when we were kids?"

"Yes, complete with the bun. Have one," Claire said as she reached into the cooler then tossed Lauren one.

Lauren unwrapped the foil and took a bite of the hot dog and groaned in happiness. "I forgot how much a cold hot dog on the beach just hits the spot."

Claire laughed. "Glad you like it because the kids want nothing to do with them. All they ask for is food from the boardwalk."

"Can't blame them," Lauren said with a shrug.

"So, how are you doing?" Claire asked, her face growing serious. "You know... after everything. We haven't talked too much about it."

Lauren lowered her sunglasses. "You mean the divorce?"

Claire glanced at the kids and back at Lauren. "Well... yeah."

"I'm doing better, I think," Lauren said as she shifted in her chair. "It was rough for a while, though."

"I'll bet."

Lauren stared out toward the ocean. "To be so invested in

someone that you build this happy life together over many years and have it all ripped out from underneath you, just ruined me. I couldn't eat. I couldn't sleep, yet I couldn't get out of bed. I could barely function at work. I think I lost twenty pounds over the past six months from that. It felt like a gut punch. The worst heartbreak of my life."

Claire nodded. "It was a gut punch to all of us. We all loved Steven. Gosh, Brian and Steven were so close. It was just shocking. We never…"

"Suspected he'd cheat on me with multiple women? Yeah, me neither. There were never any signs that he was unhappy in our marriage. None. It just didn't make sense." Lauren reached into the cooler and pulled out a can of seltzer, opened it, then took a sip.

Claire perked up. "Enough about that. Let's look to the beautiful future. I think it's great that you're here for the summer. I think you need this. Heck, I need this too."

Lauren nodded. "I do need this, and I'm sure you do too, but I sure am homesick for Vermont. We have this wonderful farmer's market in Burlington, and the bike path on Lake Champlain is like something out of a magazine. The air always seems to smell of pine trees and fire pits. Gosh, I love Vermont."

"Vermont is nice. We always loved it when visiting you. Do you have a place to live when you go back in September?" Claire asked.

Lauren shrugged. "I don't. As you know, we sold our house. He moved out first, and then I put my stuff in storage, and it lined up perfectly that I got this rental in Ocean City. It still breaks my heart, thinking about that house not being mine—or rather ours—anymore. I spent years making it a personal paradise, putting in stained glass windows, painting a custom-designed stencil on the wall in the main bedroom, planting my favorite perennials all over the yard, and having the best black-berry patch ever. If I could have afforded that house on my own, I would have bought out Steven's portion. The house prices in our neighborhood skyrocketed over the last five years."

"Did he not want to stay at the house?" Claire asked.

Lauren laughed. "He couldn't afford the house payments alone either. Heck, I make more money than he does. It just wasn't in the cards for either of us to keep the house, financially," Lauren said as she watched the lifeguards whistle at some people who were too far out in the ocean. "Let's go in the water."

"Yeah, about that. I leave ocean swimming to the kids," Claire said with a slight laugh.

Lauren lowered her sunglasses and gave Claire a look. "Just come in there with me. We won't go in far."

Claire rolled her eyes and stood up. "Fine, but the kids are coming too," she said as she waved them over.

They all walked past the many people sitting on the beach around them, to the edge of the water right by the lifeguard stand.

Claire dipped her toe in and screamed. "It's ice cold! You're out of your mind!"

Lauren laughed as she walked knee-deep into the water with Evan and Bridget, who had already found some friends in the ocean to play with, per usual. "Come on. It's refreshing," she said as she splashed some water toward Claire.

"Don't do that again," Claire said as she splashed Lauren back and followed her out past where the waves were breaking. They bobbed up and down over the gentle waves, finally relaxing and enjoying the serenity of it.

"Well, what's going on with your job?" Claire asked as Evan and Bridget swam up to her and put their arms around her neck.

"My job in events? It's practically nonexistent in the summer. People just don't seem to want to get married in the heat of the summer. I can't blame them. Then, the more corporate events are paused because they're all taking vacations. We have some other events, but there aren't many, and Rochelle will usually handle those. So, it's just another thing that worked out perfectly with me coming here this summer."

"What have you been doing for work during the summer?" Claire asked curiously. "You always seem so busy."

"You know what I did for work. We talked about it a bunch of times. I work as a freelance stage manager for Major League Baseball games at the Fenway Park. When I'm working, I stay with my college friend Maggie, who lives in Boston. I'd work a bunch of days and then go home for a few, so on and so forth. I'm actually sad to miss it this summer," Lauren said then held her nose and went underwater.

Claire laughed when Lauren bobbed back up. "You still hold your nose?"

"Yeah. It's an old habit that I can't kick," Lauren said while rubbing the salty water out of her eyes.

Claire nodded. "Oh, it's definitely old. You started that at six years old. I remember it to this day."

Lauren shrugged and smiled. "Maybe this is the summer that I learn to not do it."

CHAPTER FIVE

"Blech!" Lauren pulled cobwebs from her face and hair while walking through the small shed in her yard early the next morning. "I don't think anyone has been in here in years," she said while stepping over some rakes and hoes. "I guess I can't be too surprised, based on the horrible condition of the house." She forced out a laugh, trying to find the humor in the absurdity of it all.

She noticed a Weedwacker and large pruners hanging on a wall as well as a wheelbarrow and a lawnmower in the back. *Well, those will come in handy when I tackle the yard*, she thought.

After getting the cobwebs, dust, and grime off, she noticed two rusty old road bikes with flat tires, leaning against each other. "Well, there goes the plan for using the bikes that came with the house. Why even put that in the listing?" Lauren asked as she walked out of the shed and locked the doors behind her. She headed back inside, gave herself pigtail braids, threw a baseball cap on, then grabbed her keys, hopped into her car, and drove toward the boardwalk.

* * *

"I'll take a beach cruiser rental please. I guess for the entire day," Lauren said while handing the young man some cash.

He pointed toward the bikes. "Pick out which one you like the best, and here's the bike lock. Just have it back no later than five."

Five minutes later, she was happily riding her bright-blue beach cruiser with a basket on the boardwalk. It was her day off from the restaurant, and she couldn't have been more thrilled. She'd been a server at different restaurants during college, and it had been one of the most stressful jobs she'd ever had. On busy days, it was constant running around and getting drinks, food orders, ketchup, syrup, and napkins, along with closing out checks and finding correct change. In addition to all that madness, a table sometimes needed someone to sing "Happy Birthday," and trying to find other servers who weren't too busy to spare a minute of singing was usually impossible. She'd had dreams for years in which she suddenly remembered the table that needed ketchup had never gotten it. It haunted her. Now, she was back doing the job she'd said she'd never do again, all in the name of helping out family. Family meant a lot to her, which was the only reason she was doing it.

The sun was still waking up, so it wasn't too hot out yet, which made for the most amazing morning bike ride on the boardwalk. It wasn't crowded, as it was mostly joggers, walkers, and bicyclists out getting their morning exercise before everyone else arrived. Everything felt peaceful, especially with a slight fog in the air. Some shops were starting to open, and others already had customers forming lines. Lauren could smell sunblock, donuts, and egg-and-cheese sandwiches, while seagulls were eyeing the people walking with their food. To the right was the beach, already starting to fill in with the early birds and their beach chairs, umbrellas, and blankets. Lauren smiled as the summer breeze blew gently toward her, savoring every minute of her decision to get out and go on a bike ride. A man with his small daughter pedaled past her on the right, and under the shaded pavilion, people were enjoying their coffee and local newspapers. The atmosphere felt blissful, like she was living out one of those movie montages where everything felt perfect and right. It was like an entirely different world, being on the boardwalk early in the morning—at least, different from what she could remember since years had passed since she'd been back. It was crazy how fast life could change. A year before, she would never have expected she'd be renting a house in Ocean City, New Jersey, for an entire summer. Then again, she'd never expected to sell her beloved house in Vermont and to be divorced from Steven, either.

About two miles later, she rode up to Brown's and locked her bike on the rack. Brown's was a restaurant that also served fresh homemade donuts, complete with a separate window to order them. Lauren walked up to the window and ordered two cinnamon-sugar donuts. They were still hot, so she headed over to the railing and ate them while watching the ocean waves crash in the distance. When she was done, she licked the sugar off her fingers and got back on her bike, starting to pedal in the direction she'd come from just as a toddler ran from his parent's grasp right in front of her. She quickly steered her bike away but in the process almost crashed into another bike rider coming in the opposite direction.

"Oh my gosh. I'm so sorry," Lauren said as she stopped her bike and turned to make sure the other rider was okay. After she got a look at the man, her stomach did a flip. It was her mysterious good-looking neighbor.

"That's okay. You maneuvered around that child really well," he said while laughing and holding his surfboard with one arm. He paused after he got a good look at Lauren, realizing he recognized her, but it was too late as she had already left.

"Stupid stupid stupid," Lauren muttered to herself as she continued riding. "Why did you just speed away from him? It was obvious he had something else to say. Heck, you should have said something. He's your neighbor."

She stopped her bike in the middle of the boardwalk and looked back over her shoulder in his direction. There he was. He had locked his bike to a rack and was walking down the beach path toward the ocean, surfboard in hand. He was undeniably gorgeous. His beard was perfectly trimmed, and the muscles in his arms just glistened in the sunlight, and he surfed, owned houseplants, and had a Jeep. That was all she really knew about the guy, though he still looked vaguely familiar. She didn't even know his name.

She shook her head, trying to clear her mind, then glanced back to see him standing on the beach path, looking straight back at her. She felt like time was standing still. Maybe he was looking past her, at someone else, so she looked behind herself. Nobody was there except a couple on a bench. She looked back at him and was surprised to see him still there, looking back at her. Then she remembered that night with the woman kissing him in his sunroom. He had a girlfriend, it appeared, and Lauren was there on a bike in the middle of the boardwalk, staring at him just like that night she took a walk around the neighborhood. The guy was going to think she was a loony. *What am I doing? What is he doing?*

"Time to go, Lauren," she said to herself as she hopped back on her bike and pedaled away. *I'm not a home wrecker... and never will be. That's Steven's specialty,* she thought as she came up to a shop selling lemonade. She locked her bike up and walked over to the counter. "One large lemonade, please."

"Coming right up," the man said then juiced a couple of lemons into a tall plastic cup full of ice, sugar, and water. He shook it up, handed it to Lauren, and took her cash.

With one sip of the drink, Lauren was suddenly transported to being a kid again in Ocean City. Cute Neighbor Guy and her ex-husband were afterthoughts. She was feeling ready to tackle the day, and it had just started.

* * *

Back at the house, Lauren was geared up for an afternoon of getting dirty outside. She'd stocked up on gas for the lawnmower and Weedwacker and bought some gardening gloves. The grass and weeds were way too high for the push mower, so she went to work with the Weedwacker, starting near the fence line and making her way toward the rest of the yard.

Two hours later, the jungle was starting to look well manicured. She stood up and leaned backward to stretch her back while scanning her surroundings, marveling at how nice the space looked, even if the grass was half-dead. After everything was trimmed back, she'd gone over it again with the lawnmower and, in the process, unveiled a beautiful slate stepping stone path. That wasn't all that had been unveiled. She'd found a fig tree covered by overgrowth, a concrete bird bath, and many perennials being choked out by everything growing around them. She transplanted the perennials to the fence line, cleaned out and filled up the bird bath, and threw some fertilizer she'd found in the shed around the fig tree.

Lauren walked back into the shed and dug out an old retro lawn chair then placed it on the dock. She plopped into it and stared out at the water, watching the boaters and jet skiers coming and going and feeling quite proud of herself for tackling such a big job alone.

This is a million-dollar view right here, Lauren thought as she rested her sore muscles.

"Hey there, hon!" a voice yelled from over the fence.

Lauren turned to see Erin, her neighbor, out on her deck, enjoying drinks with some other women, all of them looking dolled up for the day.

"Oh, hi!" Lauren waved.

Erin lowered her sunglasses. "I can't believe you did all of that. We haven't seen that yard look that good in who knows how long. I was watching you out the window before my girl-friends arrived."

Lauren laughed. "That probably wasn't a pretty sight."

Erin waved her hand in the air. "I was amazed, but my gosh, you should really get a man to do all of that work for you, hon," she said, looking at her freshly done French mani-cured nails.

Lauren shrugged. "It's fine. I like a challenge here and there."

Erin smiled and took a sip of her cosmopolitan. "Why don't you come over and join us."

Lauren thought for a moment, feeling her achy body melt even more into the rickety lawn chair. "I don't know. I'm an absolute mess," she said, looking at all the pieces of grass stuck to her arms and legs.

"How about this. Go take a shower, get changed, and meet us back here in thirty minutes. Lunch will be ready by then," Erin said as she headed back inside, seemingly not taking no for an answer.

Lauren felt her stomach rumble. She hadn't eaten anything but the two donuts earlier in the morning, and she'd worked up quite the appetite. Going to Erin's was looking more and more appealing by the minute. So to the shower she went but not after one last look at all her hard work.

* * *

"There she is!" Erin squealed as Lauren approached the group of women on the deck. "And just in time. I brought out bowls of my homemade gazpacho. Here, have a seat next to Trish." She pulled a chair out.

The women all smiled and introduced themselves as Lauren took a seat at the table, ready to devour everything in front of her.

"What can I get you to drink, hon?" Erin asked.

"A glass of water is fine," Lauren said as she picked up her spoon.

Erin furrowed her brow. "Nonsense. What do you like?"

Lauren shrugged. "I guess I'll have a glass of wine. Red or white is fine if you have it."

"Perfect. I'll be right back," Erin said as she rushed inside.

Martha, one of the girlfriends, leaned in next to Lauren. "Don't feel pressured to have a *drink* if you'd rather have water."

Penny, another friend, chuckled. "She has these lunch gatherings when our husbands go out golfing together. We don't always day drink."

Trish nodded as she took a sip of her wine. "I get it. I really do. She wants to have a girls' day when the husbands are off having a guys' day. I mean, why not?"

Martha laughed. "Don't lie. We have these girls' days all the time, even when the guys aren't hanging together."

"That is true. Retirement has been quite the treat, hasn't it?" Penny said as she held her martini glass up.

"Okay, I'm back," Erin said as she placed a cold glass of sauvignon blanc in front of Lauren. "How's the gazpacho? It's my go-to summer dish to make," she said while sitting down at the table.

Lauren glanced down at the beautifully plated gazpacho in front of her. It had a swirl of olive oil with homemade croutons and sliced avocado on top. She then spooned some into her mouth, swallowed, and closed her eyes. "This is the best I've ever had."

Erin clapped her hands in excitement. "I'm so glad to hear that."

* * *

After a couple of hours of drinks, laughter, conversation, and more food (Erin had brought out homemade pound cake with whipped cream and strawberries), the husbands arrived back from their outing fully refreshed. They all walked out onto the deck, kissed their wives, and introduced themselves to Lauren.

John, Erin's husband, walked down to his fancy boat, which was tied to his dock. "Anybody want to go for a boat ride on the bay?"

The ladies all glanced at each other, then they all nodded. "Yes, most definitely," Erin said as she got up to take away the dishes.

"I can help you with that," Lauren said as she started clearing the table.

"You're too sweet," Erin said as they walked inside together with dirty dishes and glasses. "Did you want to go out on the boat with us?"

Lauren shrugged. "Well... I don't want to impose."

Erin rolled her eyes. "Please, you're wonderful. You had us all laughing out there at the table. I'm pretty sure everyone would love if you came, hon."

Lauren smiled. "Well, if you put it that way. I guess count me in."

Once everything was loaded into the dishwasher, they headed back outside to see everyone had already boarded the boat and was waiting on them.

Derek, Trish's husband, turned up the radio to some seventies disco song as Lauren and Erin got on board and found a seat next to each other in the front. John backed the boat out then slowly drove it past the houses along the bay.

Erin's eyes widened as they passed Lauren's rental then the mysterious neighbor's house next door. "Have you met Matt yet?"

Lauren glanced at Erin. "Matt?"

"Yeah, him..." Erin said, pointing at his house.

"Not... really," Lauren said as she stared at his yard, never really having seen it before since her yard had a six-foot fence all around it. His property was gorgeous, with some type of tiki bar in the corner and a seating area with a fire pit in the center. There were white string lights hung from tall wood posts in the corners and colorful blooming perennials and ornamental grasses in every nook and corner. It looked like something out of a magazine.

"Not really?" Erin asked curiously.

"I've had a couple run-ins with him but no formal introductions yet," Lauren said as the boat continued on past more houses.

"He's a really nice guy. I don't know too much about him, just talking to him here and there, but I do know he helps a lot of the neighbors out from time to time," Erin said with a smile.

"Oh yeah? Like with what?" Lauren asked, growing more interested in the conversation by the second.

"He would check on people's pets when they were out of town, bring in their mail, you know, stuff like that. Oh, there was this one time, Sue, who lives a couple houses down, fell down her front steps and tore her quad tendon when nobody was home. Poor thing kept trying to stand up and couldn't do it. She just lay there. He happened to be driving by and noticed something was wrong. He got her into his car and drove her to the ER. By then, her husband had arrived, and he couldn't have been more grateful that someone was looking out for his wife."

Lauren smiled, all the while feeling her heart sink a little. Of course someone like Matt had a girlfriend. There weren't many women that would let someone that gorgeous and kind be single for too long. Then she thought about Steven, and her throat started to feel like it was closing. She had viewed him as this amazing partner all of those years, and it had all turned out to be a big lie, a big waste of time that she'd never get back. Now, she was forty-three years old, and suddenly, she wasn't sure if she'd trust another man again.

John accelerated the boat. "Okay, everyone. Hold onto your hats," he said as they moved out of the no-wake zone.

"Here comes my favorite part of the boat ride," Erin said as she nudged Lauren playfully.

Lauren smiled as she looked around at everyone on the boat, the wind whipping their hair wildly, all the while laughing and admiring the views. They were fully enjoying being out on the water with friends in sunny Ocean City. It was that moment that she had to pinch herself. Life was starting to feel a lot more exciting lately and, dare she say, happier.

CHAPTER SIX

"Good morning, Lauren," Mr. Young said as he sat in his usual spot at the counter at Chipper's.

"Good morning. Good to see you, Mr. Young," Lauren said with a smile as she walked in at eight, finding her way to the hot coffee-pot behind the counter. She filled up a cup for herself.

Mr. Young took a bite of his food as he sat arm-to-arm with other customers who were all enjoying their plates of breakfast. "Don't ever get rid of these homemade cinnamon rolls," he said, pointing at his plate.

Doug, another customer, nodded in agreement. "You can't get them this good anywhere else. Not even in Philly. Heck, not even in New York City. I travel a lot for work, and these are the best I've ever had."

Lauren leaned on the counter and took a sip of her coffee. "I hear this a lot. I remember eating them as a kid when we'd visit Ocean City and loving them even then. They're so gooey in the middle, and the frosting is out of this world. It's my grandmother's secret recipe."

Joe pushed the swinging door open from the kitchen, interrupting their conversation in the process. "Lauren, do you mind dropping these two baskets off to the two booths all the way to the right?"

Lauren took the baskets. "Dad, it's been two weeks. I know the table numbers now."

Joe chuckled. "Okay, fine. Tables three and four."

"Perfect," Lauren said as she glanced down at the baskets while she walked them over. Chipper's was known not only for their cinnamon rolls but also for their muffin baskets chock-full of homemade muffins, croissants, and cinnamon-raisin bread. On the side were house-made jams and honey butter to spread on top. It wasn't something you'd think to find at an old-school greasy spoon restaurant but more so at an upscale brunch spot. That was the appeal of Chipper's, though. It pleased both types of crowds, but lately the restaurant just seemed to be a stressful mess for both the workers and the customers as her family went through the growing pains of learning to run it. It'd been two weeks since Lauren started working at Chipper's, and she could plainly see it was running anything but smoothly. She had taken notes on what needed to be fixed and even worked out a feasible plan, but her dad didn't want to hear it. He was dead set on making the restaurant work his way.

The bell on the door chimed as Claire walked in with surprise all over her face after seeing Lauren there. "What are you doing here? Remember I told you I'd fill in so you could have the day off? You've worked ten days in a row. That's too much."

Lauren shrugged as she took the coffee-pot and refilled some customer's cups. "I don't know. I didn't have anything else to do, so I figured I'd pop in."

Claire rolled her eyes. "Anything else to do? You're down the shore in the summer. There's a million things to do. Plus, Mom is coming in to work for a little bit too."

Lauren nodded as she set the coffee pot down. "I guess you're right. Maybe I'll head out, then."

"Yes, I think that would be a good idea," Claire said as she walked behind the counter, then she said hi to the cooks.

Lauren said goodbye to Mr. Young and the other customers she had struck up a conversation with and headed back through the kitchen to let her dad know she was leaving, when she noticed Bobby, one of the cooks, walking through a mystery door with a stack of to-go boxes.

"What's in there?" Lauren asked.

"Oh that?" Bobby asked, pointing behind himself. "That's where we keep dry storage."

Lauren's dad cut in. "Past the dry storage is the little store your grandparents used to run alongside the restaurant."

"Oh. How could I forget? I remember that shop. I used to love spending time there as a kid," Lauren said as she thought of the happy memories of running through the aisles and playing hide-and-seek with her sister and cousins.

Lauren's dad nudged her. "Go check it out, then," he said as he handed her some keys from his back pocket. "Though I'm warning you it might be a mess in there. I don't think anyone has touched it in years. It hasn't been open since the nineties."

Lauren felt a thrill run through her as she opened the door and walked through the dry storage area until she got to another door. It was locked, so she unlocked it with one of the keys her father had given her and opened it to a very dark room with a strong scent of cardboard boxes, dried flowers, and old books. She was instantly transported back to the eighties and nineties just from the smell. It made her giddy as she searched the wall blindly for a light switch, then she finally found it. The lights went on, and Lauren stared in disbelief. It was like time had stood still in the store. Except for all of the dust and a bunch of vines that had somehow made their way through a crack in the window, everything was exactly as she last remembered it, down to the fully stocked shelves.

Lauren felt her heart start to pound as she walked slowly

through the aisles, taking everything in little by little. The aisle with hundreds of different ribbons was still there. Thick ribbons, thin ribbons, printed ribbons, and solid-colored ribbons lined the shelves, and mixed in were the house-made bows that people would often get made for their wreaths, swags, garlands, and so forth. Lauren smiled as she remembered Beverly, a woman who worked there making bows back in the late eighties and nineties. Customers would pick out their ribbon, and she'd whip out a big, extravagant bow with many layers then twist wire on the bottom so it could be attached to something easily.

Lauren came to the aisles with the wreaths, garlands, and swags and all the things you could decorate them with, like plastic fruit and vegetables, silk flowers, little wooden animals and mushrooms, beads, and nautical items like anchors and ship steering wheels. Of course, since they were at the beach, you couldn't forget the decorative miniature flip-flops, beach balls, and ocean waves. It was an endless assortment of items to choose from. Whether you were decorating for a baby shower or Halloween, they had it.

As she maneuvered her way through the store, the memories came flooding back as she approached her favorite section. It was the party supply aisle, complete with other odds and ends like foil pencils, Paddington Bear erasers, vintage stickers upon stickers, and old children's books. Lauren picked up some eighties Rainbow Brite party hats then walked over to look at a pack of Strawberry Shortcake napkins. She glanced at the price sticker: ninety-nine cents. If only prices had stayed that way.

"You in here?" Claire yelled from the front of the store.

"Yeah, in the back," Lauren said as she pulled down some GI Joe party streamers.

"I thought you went home, but Dad said you were back here. We slowed down a bit, so I wanted to take a look myself." Claire gasped when she saw about fifteen Pound Puppies and

Kitties still in the boxes. "What in the world!" she said as she grabbed one and held it to her chest. "Remember when I had my tonsils removed when I was seven? They let me bring one stuffed animal with me to the hospital. I chose Bowser, my Pound Puppy. It was such a comfort to me, then Mom and Dad threw him out when I went off to college.

Lauren shook her head. "They threw everything out. All of our childhood dolls…"

"I would have liked to give them to my children. Heck, those things would have sold well on ebay too," Claire said, feeling annoyed.

Lauren sighed as she looked around the store. "I just can't believe our grandparents left all of this dead stock in here. It's like they fully stocked the store with hundreds of dollars of items then shut it down, preserving it in time."

Claire shook her head. "I know. I mean, not even a closing sale or something? I guess they didn't need the money, so they didn't care."

"It's just absolutely incredible. I could spend hours in here, looking at all of this amazing stuff," Lauren said as she walked around coming to an area against the wall behind the shelves. "You've got to be kidding me."

"What?" Claire asked as she followed Lauren.

"They have extra stock for all of the stocked items on the shelves back here. *Tons* of it," Lauren said as her widened eyes scanned the high shelves.

"This is bonkers, but it's probably starting to pick up in the restaurant. I'd better get back there. We'll talk later," Claire said as she hurried out of the store, still clutching the Pound Puppy.

Lauren stood by herself deep in thought, trying to remember every little bit of how the store used to be run. Would a place like this survive in today's world?

* * *

That evening, the whole family went out for dinner in Somers Point at Joe's favorite, the Crab Trap. It was a busy summer night, but they managed to get there at a good time, as there wasn't a wait yet.

"Follow me this way," the host said as Joe, Nancy, Lauren, Claire, Brian, Bridget, and Evan trailed behind her. They had pushed some tables together in the middle of the restaurant for their party, which worked out nicely.

The Crab Trap had been around many years, just like Chipper's, and was a favorite of both locals and vacationers. On the wooden tables sat votive candle holders with a ship etched on the glass, and the inside of the restaurant had this comforting nautical vibe to it.

Lauren glanced at the menu before putting it down and looking at her father. "So, you like the crab cakes here?"

"Yes, can't beat 'em. The deviled crab cakes in particular," Joe said as he set his menu down, already knowing what he was going to get.

"Then I guess I'll get that," Lauren said as she glanced at Claire talking to the kids, trying to figure out what they would eat off the menu.

Ten minutes later, they had their drinks and had ordered, and Joe was trying to talk over everyone's conversations.

"Can I have all of your attention for a moment?"

Nobody seemed to hear him, as Claire, Lauren, and Brian were busy laughing about some absurd situation Brian had gotten himself into earlier in the day.

"Ahem!" Joe said as he cleared his throat.

"What's up, Dad?" Claire asked, feeling slightly annoyed by the interruption.

"Your mother and I have something important to discuss tonight," Joe said as he glanced at Nancy, who gave him an approving nod. That seemed to get everyone at the table's attention, including the kids.

"As you know, running this restaurant has been quite the

feat. Your mother and I have been feeling overworked and stressed with it all. It's not exactly the relaxing type of job that most people take on after retirement," Joe said.

Lauren nodded. "That's exactly what I've been saying the whole time. It's too much to handle."

Nancy cut in. "Anyway, your father had a doctor's appointment the other day, and his blood pressure is through the roof. They had to increase his medication dosage. On top of that, they didn't like the looks of his EKG this time around. They asked if anything has been causing stress in his life, and we brought up the restaurant."

Joe shook his head. "As you know, stress is a killer... literally. My doctor let me know that up front... and well... we're starting to think that we need to figure something out for Chipper's, or it will literally be the death of me, even if it's only open in the summer. If I want a job during retirement, it's going to have to be part-time and relaxing. Working at the restaurant is anything but that. For one, I'm putting in sixty-hour weeks."

Nancy sighed. "We're just so worried about letting the community down. You know how beloved the restaurant is. Not only that, but it's your grandparents' legacy. They built this restaurant to be what it is today."

Joe gulped. "Anyway, it just so happens that we had a nice gentleman come into Chipper's early this morning before we opened. Tony was his name. He explained that he's interested in purchasing Chipper's—"

"What?" Lauren cut in. "He wants to purchase Chipper's? To do what with it?"

Nancy shrugged. "We're assuming to run it. Restaurants change ownership all of the time. It's not uncommon. It wouldn't be within the family anymore, but it would at least still be open to the public."

Claire shook her head. "Wow. I mean, I knew running this

restaurant wasn't the best idea for you two, but I didn't think we'd be having this conversation so early in the game."

Tears started welling up in Joe's eyes. "It hasn't been an easy thing to discuss. I feel like I'd be letting down my parents, may their souls rest in peace, but Lauren is right. We should be relaxing on the beach and enjoying our retirement, not working ourselves into the ground like we did so many years prior. I'd like to live long enough to enjoy these years. Not to mention, I don't have any more siblings that can take it over. My brother did his time at the restaurant and wants nothing more to do with it, and my sister is happy with her life out in California. Can't say I blame them. Then there's you two both living out of state with your own careers."

Lauren was suddenly conflicted. The last couple of weeks, being at the restaurant had really grown on her. It was starting to feel like the set of *Cheers* whenever she was there, knowing all of the regulars and hearing their stories. Dare she say it was starting to feel like home.

"Well, we want you two around as long as possible, and it sounds like stepping away from the restaurant is what is best for your health and sanity. I fully support your decision," Claire said just as their salads and bread baskets arrived at the table.

"Thank you, Claire. We appreciate that," Nancy said as she glanced at Lauren. "But how do you feel about it, Lauren?"

Lauren stared off into the distance in thought, not really sure how she felt about it all. She definitely agreed that her parents should step away, but selling the family business to strangers just seemed so scary. What if the new owners changed up the menu and made it completely different or ripped out the charming vintage booths and put in boring basic new ones? What would happen to the employees? Would they keep their jobs? If they did, would the management be just as kind and accommodating as her parents had been? There were endless possibilities of how selling the business could go south—too many to name. But was that the risk you took to move on from something? Perhaps it was.

CHAPTER SEVEN

Lauren stood on her yoga mat at eight thirty a.m., watching the waves crash in front of her while doing the reverse warrior pose with the rest of the yoga class. She glanced over at Claire next to her, who was struggling to maintain her balance.

"Okay, let's go into downward dog," the instructor said, then the class started moving into the new pose.

Claire sighed in relief as she put both of her hands on the mat. Downward-facing dog was a much simpler pose for her, especially on the uneven sand.

It was a beautiful morning in Ocean City, and it was the first yoga-on-the-beach class for both Lauren and Claire. The sun was waking up, and there was a morning fog over the beach that it made it feel that much more grounding and peaceful.

Within thirty minutes, they were finishing up the class with some cool-down poses that had them lying with their backs on the mats, and Lauren felt as though her body could sink right into the sand. She was a sweaty mess, and her muscles ached, but she felt completely relaxed. The sound of the ocean waves had almost lulled her into sleep when a shadow appeared over her, blocking the sun.

"Class is done. You ready to hit up the farmer's market?" Claire asked with her rolled-up yoga mat under her arm.

Lauren sat up and reached for her toes, getting one last stretch in. "I'm down. Maybe we can find something to eat for breakfast, because I'm starving."

* * *

Fifteen minutes later, they arrived at the crowded market full of vendors under pop-up tents on Asbury Avenue.

Lauren's eyes lit up as she maneuvered around all the people walking with their newly purchased goodies. "This reminds me of our beloved farmer's market in Vermont."

Claire nodded as she watched two people walk by with big bouquets of flowers. "It does, but this market definitely seems bigger."

Lauren stopped to look at a produce stand chock-full of Jersey-grown zucchini, summer squash, cucumbers, lettuce, and tomatoes, among other things. A younger couple greeted people as they looked over the vegetables and fruit, and it appeared that they were selling items that they grew on their little farm.

"Hi there. I'll take a couple zucchinis and three red tomatoes," Lauren said to the woman as she got out her wallet, feeling thrilled to support a small business.

After she'd filled her canvas tote up with her produce, they made their way to the homemade bread stand and purchased two loaves of sourdough—one for each of them—and then headed off to find something for breakfast.

"How do you feel about tacos?" Claire asked as they approached a vendor selling Mexican food.

"For breakfast?" Lauren asked, surprised.

"Why not? It's only a few hours till lunch anyway," Claire said as she stared at the menu.

Lauren shrugged. "Well, I can always go for tacos, I guess.

I'll take two chicken tacos, please," she told the man working the stand.

"Make that four with some guacamole on the side," Claire chimed in with a wink at Lauren.

Moments later, they were standing off to the side, devouring their delicious tacos. "These are insanely good," Lauren said as she finished her last bite.

Claire shook her head as she took a sip of her drink. "Oh, we're coming back here next week for more. They must marinate that chicken in something incredible. I can't put my finger on what, though… and that guacamole was so fresh. I've gotta take Brian here. He'll love it."

Lauren pointed at a stand selling artwork. "Let's go see what they have," she said as she led Claire through the crowd.

As they approached the different paintings and photographs for sale, Lauren glanced at the stand next to it, noticing a man sitting in a chair behind a table with some small plants and clothing for sale. She widened her eyes and grabbed Claire's arm, pulling her aside. "Look," she said, motioning with her head discreetly.

Claire immediately turned to see Matt taking cash from a customer who was buying a succulent. "Your neighbor is here," she blurted out.

Lauren quickly hurried off and ducked under a tent selling pies, dragging Claire with her. "Did you really just scream that? Did he hear you? I'm mortified," she said, trying to disguise herself behind a tent flap.

Claire laughed as she looked back at Matt. "He didn't hear me over all this noise out here. He's helping a customer. I'm guessing you haven't talked to him yet, by the way you're acting."

Lauren shrugged. "Honestly, we must work different hours as I haven't seen him much since that first week that I moved in."

Claire pushed Lauren out of the pie tent. "Why don't you go introduce yourself. Now seems like the perfect time."

Lauren swallowed hard as she was now in the middle of the street with people walking past her on both sides. Matt's tent was only fifteen feet away, and suddenly her stomach felt completely sick. She started walking toward Matt's stand but only glanced at it as she passed it and went to the homemade soap vendor next to him.

Claire rolled her eyes as Lauren picked up a rosemary-mint bar of soap and smelled it. "Really? Are you in middle school? If you don't go talk to him, I will. This is absurd."

Lauren put the soap down and turned to look Claire in the eyes. "Why do you want me to talk to him so bad?"

Claire sighed. "Because I do. It's the neighborly thing to do. Heck, you've already hung out with the neighbors on the other side... and he's cute."

"And most likely taken..." Lauren said as she took a deep breath. "Fine." She walked over to Matt's tent, pretending to look at some shirts with her back to him.

"Those are hand-painted. Beauties, aren't they?" Matt asked with a smile.

Lauren adjusted her hair as she turned to face Matt. "Yes, they're so unique. I love them."

Matt's face started to turn red as he realized who he was talking to, but his smile remained. "Hey... You're my—"

"New neighbor. I saw you a couple times the week I moved in," Lauren cut in, unable to hide her smile back.

"That's right. I actually stopped by to introduce myself the other day, but you weren't home," Matt said as he rang another customer up.

Claire, who was pretending to look at some plants, stared at Lauren with widened eyes, covering her mouth to disguise her smile.

"Oh, really? What day was that?" Lauren asked, now feeling more comfortable.

"I think it was Sunday evening," he said as he handed a customer their change.

"Anyway, I'm Matt," he said while extending his hand for Lauren to shake.

"I'm Lauren. Nice to meet you, Matt. Great stand you have," she said while their hands lingered a few seconds after the shake.

Matt nodded as he kept his eyes on Lauren. "This is just a little thing I like to do. It gets me out of the shop on Wednesdays. A change of scenery is nice."

"Your shop?" Claire blurted out.

Lauren laughed. "Matt, this is my sister, Claire."

"Nice to meet you, Claire. Yes, you two should come by the shop on the boardwalk sometime. It's called Jungle Surf. It's both a surf shop and a plant store in one."

Claire bit her lip as she looked over at Lauren. "Well, that's pretty cool. I'm sure we'll find some time to go check it out. In the meantime, I'll take these two aloe plants."

"These will be great for some after-sun care when you get home from the beach," Matt said as he took Claire's cash and then proceeded to put the plants into a small cardboard box.

Lauren tried to hide her chuckle. Claire had never kept one houseplant alive ever, including the hard-to-kill cactus.

"Well, I guess I'll see you around," Lauren said as she led the way out of the tent.

"Yes... I hope so," Matt muttered quietly but loud enough for Claire to hear, making her ears perk up.

* * *

After dropping off Claire and getting her goodies from the farmer's market into her house, Lauren decided to head over to Chipper's to check on things. It'd been a few weeks since their parents had the discussion about turning the restaurant over to someone else, and everything still seemed to be up in the air.

"Well, look who it is," Joe said as Lauren walked into a busy and noisy restaurant.

The cooks were behind the counter on the griddle, flipping pancakes, sausage, bacon, and eggs, and it just felt so homey and wonderful to be in there. You couldn't be sad or mad when you were at Chipper's. The atmosphere wouldn't allow it. The food smelled incredible, and conversations and laughter could be heard from every corner.

"Tony, I'd like you to meet my daughter, Lauren," Joe said as Tony was revealed, standing behind a rolling cart of glasses that had just been pushed inside the kitchen.

Lauren was taken aback. *This* was Tony? The one who wanted to buy the restaurant? He looked to be her age, maybe a tad younger, wearing a high-end suit. He had an old-school Italian way about him that was both abrasive and charming as he looked Lauren up and down and smiled. "So, this is *the* Lauren. I've heard a lot about you," he said as he flashed his full paper-white-veneer smile and held his hand out for a handshake.

Lauren shook his hand then crossed her arms. "Dad, what exactly are you telling strangers about me?"

Joe cleared his throat. "Just how hard-working and motivated you are… and how you picked yourself up by your bootstraps after the divorce."

Lauren widened her eyes as she stared at her father. "Dad, that's a little personal. I'd prefer—"

Tony put his hand on Lauren's shoulder. "It's okay. He meant no harm. It just casually came up when I brought up my divorce during our discussion."

Lauren wasn't buying it. He had the appeal of a used-car salesman at this point.

Joe cut in. "Anyway, we're getting the ball rolling with Tony purchasing the restaurant. Your mother should be arriving any minute to go over some things regarding the sale."

A couple of regular customers overheard and dropped their forks onto their plates out of shock.

Joe motioned toward the door. "Let's take this conversation outside, shall we?"

Tony, Lauren, and Joe all walked outside, away from the customers.

Tony looked out toward the beach in front of Chipper's. "This is prime real estate right here. You don't see many restaurants right off the beach like this. This is a dream of mine, to run a local dining spot in Ocean City."

Lauren nodded. "My grandparents built this restaurant from the ground up. It's very sentimental to us. What kind of restaurant would you be running? Would it stay the same?"

Tony thought for a moment. "Well, I guess it would stay the same. Those details are a little fuzzy right now, though."

Lauren shifted her eyes, not really liking the response, but her dad didn't seem to think anything of it. "I'm sure you'll figure out all of those details and let us know prior to the sale," Joe said as he flashed an excited smile.

Tony looked down at his Rolex and adjusted it on his wrist. "I sure will."

"Great. Let me just go check on a couple things, and I'll be right back. Don't go anywhere," Joe said as he hurried back inside.

Tony turned to Lauren, who was staring at an adorable family eating at a table under an umbrella. The couple had twin toddlers in high chairs, and each parent was cutting up some eggs and pancakes for them and placing it on their trays. The toddlers each took a handful and placed a tiny bit in their mouth, with the rest of it falling to the ground. Lauren couldn't help but smile.

Tony scoffed. "Kids are so messy at restaurants, no? Food everywhere. It's a good thing they're sitting outside. I'm sure some ants will have a feast pretty soon."

Lauren rolled her eyes. "Well, we are a family restaurant. It comes with the territory."

"Right, right," Tony said with a forced laugh as he took out his car key fob and locked the doors on his Mercedes-Benz. He turned to face Lauren. "You doing anything later tonight?"

Lauren paused. "Um… Not as of right now. Why?"

"I've got two tickets to a comedy show in Atlantic City. I was thinking maybe dinner at one of those nice steak houses beforehand," Tony said as he looked down at his suit jacket and wiped off a few stray hairs.

"Yeah, I don't think so. That's sounding too much like a date," Lauren said as she walked over to a table and stacked up the dirty dishes sitting on it.

Tony followed her. "Well, we don't have to call it a date. Maybe just call it a business meeting. You can tell me all about the restaurant… for research purposes."

Lauren laughed. "I've only been working at Chipper's for four weeks, and before that, I haven't been here since I was a kid. I've been living in Vermont."

Tony nodded. "That's totally fine. I'm sure you've learned enough in the past month to get the feel of the place. I want to know what I'm potentially getting into. Well, *most likely* getting into at this point. I know for a fact that I want to buy Chipper's."

Lauren started to feel sick as she carried the stack of dishes toward the front door. It was all starting to feel real. This guy was dead set on buying the place. Was it a good thing?

"Tony, I don't really feel comfortable going out with a stranger to Atlantic City. I have to respectfully decline."

Tony bit his lip. "I get it. How about this? Maybe a casual lunch at Piccini here in Ocean City tomorrow? Nothing crazy. I just want to pick your brain," he said as he held the door open for Lauren.

Lauren walked to the kitchen and set the dishes down then glanced over at her father. He had taken a seat in a chair that was placed next to the walk-in freezer, and his eyes were closed and his head leaning against the wall.

"Dad, are you okay?" Lauren asked.

Joe opened his eyes. "I think so. I just got a little dizzy after I leaned down to pick up some fallen silverware. I thought I was going to faint. Thankfully, Richie noticed and brought a chair over for me. I'm pretty sure it's from my blood pressure medication dosage being increased."

Lauren felt her heart sink. Maybe it was best that she go on a little business lunch date with Tony because, with her dad's health ailments, it was looking like they needed to figure out the fate of the restaurant quickly.

CHAPTER EIGHT

Lauren met Tony at Piccini on West Avenue at noon the next day. Having lunch with him wasn't exactly her idea of a good time, but if this man was going to purchase the family's restaurant, she'd better get to the bottom of his intentions.

She walked inside the restaurant and immediately spotted Tony in the back corner at a table for two. He was in a suit jacket again, his dark hair slicked back, and he appeared to be on an important phone call as he stood up and faced the window to continue the discussion.

Lauren walked behind him and cleared her throat to get his attention.

"Oh, hey there," Tony said, turning to see Lauren. He held his finger up to her, signaling to give him a minute. "Tommy, I've got to go. We'll continue this conversation later. We have a lot to discuss."

"Did I come at a bad time?" Lauren asked as she took a seat at the table.

Tony put his phone in his pocket and sat across from Lauren. "No, of course not. I was just catching up with a friend of mine—You look nice today," Tony said as a smile formed on his face.

"Uh… thanks?" Lauren said, feeling a little taken aback by the compliment. "Well, let's figure out what we want to eat, order, and then get to talking about the restaurant. I want to know exactly what you plan to do with Chipper's."

Tony quickly browsed the menu and unbuttoned the top button of his white shirt after feeling his neck start to sweat. "Yeah… we'll definitely go over *all* of that."

A waitress came over and greeted them. "What can I get you two?"

Lauren smiled. "I think we can order everything right now. I'll have an unsweetened iced tea and the sautéed-chicken-and-spinach sandwich."

"And I'll have the same," Tony said as he handed his menu over to the waitress.

Lauren shifted her eyes. "Did you even look at the menu?"

Tony laughed. "Nope. I trust your judgment, though."

"You could have said you weren't ready."

Tony shrugged. "I know you want to get out of here. Might as well keep it moving."

Lauren suddenly felt bad for him. Was it *that* obvious she didn't want to be there? She tried to lighten the mood. "Did you end up going to that comedy show in Atlantic City last night?"

Tony nodded. "I did. I took my mom. We had a blast."

"That's sweet of you," Lauren said as she tried to hide the smile forming on her face.

"Well, you know. I do what I can," Tony said as he looked down at the time on his Rolex.

"I guess we can get into it now. Tell me your plans for the restaurant," Lauren said as she leaned her head on her hands, giving her full attention to him.

Tony leaned back in his chair then looked at the ceiling, seemingly getting his thoughts together. His strong-smelling cologne wafted through the air. Lauren couldn't decide if the musky scent was nice or obnoxious.

"My parents came from Italy to the United States for a better life in the 1970s. They started a restaurant called Celeste's, named after my mother, in Atlantic City with some of the best Italian food around. It was right off the beach, like Chipper's. Man, I can still smell the food cooking in that restaurant to this day. You couldn't just show up. You had to have a reservation to get in, and they were booked months in advance. They opened the books for the summer in February, and everyone would stand in a long line spanning multiple blocks to get their summer reservations in. It was a spectacle. Not only that, but the celebrities that came to Atlantic City always wanted to eat there. They had a private back room just for them and even a back entrance. The celebrities loved that because they were able to enjoy themselves without the paparazzi knowing. You should have seen it."

Lauren was so captivated by the story that she barely noticed that their food and drinks had already arrived.

Tony stopped talking and took a bite of his chicken-and-spinach sandwich. "Wow. You know how to order. This is fantastic."

Lauren took a bite of hers and swallowed. "It's my favorite. I think it's the warm balsamic honey mustard dressing and the red onions that really give it that flavor punch, you know?"

Tony nodded as he took a sip of his iced tea. "It's definitely that."

"So, tell me more about your parents' restaurant. I'm intrigued," Lauren said then took another bite.

Tony smiled and stared at the ceiling again then focused his eyes back on Lauren. "Well, they were known for having the best chicken parm around. Cooked perfectly with a crispy exterior. The pasta and marinara was made in house, so it was fresh and flavorful. I mean, everything was good. My mom's tiramisu, the cannoli... I could go on and on. I worked there for many years with them in the summers during high school and college and then after college. Anyway, I bring their restaurant up because twenty years ago, it burned down to the studs overnight. Years of work and memories gone like that. It was devastating, to say the least, but I've always had this dream of running my own restaurant since."

Lauren paused. "I'm sorry to hear about your parent's restaurant, but Chipper's seems so different from Celeste's. Is that really the type of restaurant you want to own? Perhaps an Italian restaurant is the way to go."

Tony fumbled on his words. "Well, I really just love working in a restaurant. I'm not looking to necessarily start another Italian restaurant. We already have a ton of them around here in South Jersey. Plus, if that desire strikes me, I can start an Italian restaurant elsewhere."

Lauren breathed a sigh of relief. "That's great to hear. So... if you purchased Chipper's, would you change a lot about it?"

Tony cracked his knuckles. "Maybe some little things like adding a few extra menu items, perhaps updating the kitchen... stuff like that."

"Really? So, you would pretty much be leaving it how it is?" Lauren asked, surprised.

Tony took the last bite of his sandwich and nodded. "Pretty much."

"Good, because that's super important to me and my family. Like your parents, my grandparents built this restaurant from the ground up, and we'd like it to continue on. My dad was given this restaurant, and he and my mother can't handle the stress of it. I'm glad to see it would go into good hands if you bought it," Lauren said as she looked away, feeling tears welling up in her eyes.

Tony looked down at his watch again then immediately held his hand up to the waitress. "We'll take our check."

They left the restaurant and ended up in the parking lot, where Lauren shook Tony's hand. "Well, I'm glad we talked. I'm feeling better about everything. Thank you so much for lunch. I'm sure I'll be seeing you around," she said as she started walking toward the sidewalk.

Tony shifted his eyes and yelled out toward her, "Did you walk here?"

"Yeah. I need the exercise!" Lauren yelled back.

"It's going into the nineties today. How about I give you a ride home?" Tony asked.

"I'll be fine," Lauren said as she started walking, but the truth was she was already sweating, and there wasn't a lick of shade in sight. "You know what..." She turned back around. "I'll take you up on that offer."

About eight minutes later, they had pulled up to her rental on Bay Road with Frank Sinatra playing.

Tony put the car in park as Lauren turned toward him. "It was great having lunch with you, and I know I said it already, but you looked beautiful," Tony said.

Lauren blushed. "Thank you, but that's not appropriate to say for a business lunch."

"Well, can I say it if I take you out on a date next?" Tony asked.

Lauren was caught off guard by the question. Had she been naive about his intentions with today's lunch the whole time? Was this all a ploy to go on a date with her? Or was it something else?

* * *

"Finally, all of us out for an evening on the boardwalk," Claire said as Bridget and Evan ran ahead of her, Brian, and Lauren toward the rides. "The kids have been talking about going to Wonderland all week."

"Remember when we would spend all evening going on each of the rides?" Lauren asked as they followed behind the kids toward the ticket booth.

Claire laughed. "How can I forget? We each ate an entire

funnel cake then went on the Tilt-A-Whirl, where I had never felt sicker in my life."

Lauren smirked at Brian. "She had to run off the ride and find the nearest trash can. Luckily, there was one close by."

Brian playfully nudged Claire. "That sounds accurate."

Claire laughed and nudged him back. "He says that because we met in college at a party where I had too much to drink. I was sick in the bathroom, and Brian felt sorry for me. He brought me a bottle of water and stood outside the door the entire time while my friends were busy flirting with guys at the party."

Lauren nodded. "Oh, I remember the story well."

Brian laughed. "Right? How could you forget? She only retells it every chance she can get."

Claire crossed her arms. "Ha, ha. Funny, you guys."

Brian put his arms around Claire's shoulders. "We only tease you because we love you."

They purchased tickets, and Bridget and Evan were dead set on starting off on the flying swings.

"Did you guys want to go on the swings too?" Claire asked, holding up some tickets.

Lauren shifted her eyes. "I don't know. They scare me a little."

Claire grabbed Lauren's hand and followed behind the kids and Brian. "Let's do it for old times' sake."

Lauren was now somehow sitting on a swing, getting secured in with the bar, and starting to feel very nervous as they all waited for the ride to start.

"It's going to be great. Just sit back, and enjoy the breeze and sights," Claire said to Lauren.

Suddenly, the dance music got louder, and the swings started slowly going around in a circle as they rose higher.

"Okay. This is rather nice," Lauren said as she looked around at the park.

Then the swings rose even higher and went faster and faster until the entire park was a blur.

Lauren could feel her stomach tie up in knots as she tried to catch her breath and calm herself. "Just breathe. Just breathe."

The ride finally ended, and when Lauren got off, she was ready to kiss the ground.

"Wasn't that great?" Claire asked as they exited together.

Lauren laughed. "No. I'm never getting on that ride again. I thought I was going to hurl on everyone below us the entire time, and now my stomach is not happy with me."

Claire smirked. "Well, I guess it truly was like old times, then, huh?"

"You could say that," Lauren said as she looked out toward the boardwalk. "I think I'm going to go on a little walk to settle my stomach. If I'm not back by the time the kids are done with the rides, give me a call."

Claire smiled. "Sounds good. Sorry about your stomach. That's my fault."

"It's okay," Lauren said as she headed back onto the busy boards.

She started walking and immediately felt better. The sound of the ocean was so peaceful, and all the different people out and about and the brightly lit stores immediately distracted her from her uneasy stomach.

Then there it was: Jungle Surf, Matt's shop that he had mentioned. It looked packed inside, and Lauren hesitated as she thought about whether she wanted to go inside or not. Ultimately, she decided to stop in.

She walked into what felt like a tropical paradise, like a completely different world from what was going on on the rest of the boardwalk. Different houseplants like philodendrons and pothos hung from the ceiling, and there was a huge potted monstera plant on the floor, as well as small succulents on tables and shelves. Reggae played on the speakers, and there was a large manmade waterfall in the center of the room. Along with the plants were racks of surf-style clothing and sandals and, of course, surfboards. On the tables with the plants were beautiful plant books and surfing books, bottles of sunblock, and locally made jewelry.

Lauren maneuvered around some people to look at a succulent in the back corner of the room. Really, she wanted a spot where she could scan the store to see if Matt was actually working. Her heart sank a little when she realized he wasn't there. She took one last look around and started to head back toward the boardwalk when a voice made her stop.

"Hey, Lauren!"

Lauren felt her stomach twist up again as she turned around to see Matt walking from a back room with a shoe box that he promptly gave to a customer. He had remembered her name.

"Oh, hi… Matt. I was on the boardwalk and thought I'd finally check out your little spot here," she said as she touched a huge monstera leaf.

Matt smiled as he towered over her. He had to be six-four or six-five. "What do you think?"

Lauren looked around the room, nodding her head, then met Matt's eyes. "I'm honestly blown away. I feel like I'm in a different world in here. It's very unique to see how you blended a surf and plant shop in one. I mean, the books, the sunblock, even the little sunset paintings. It's perfectly melded together for this amazing shopping experience."

Matt blushed and leaned his arm on a support beam. "Wow. That's the highest compliment. Thank you. I appreciate that."

Lauren watched as a group of teenagers walked past them toward the beach-style dresses for sale. "My sister and her husband and kids are over at Wonderland, going on the rides. I felt a little sick on one and ended up walking the boards."

Matt laughed. "Which ride?"

Lauren put her hand on her stomach. "The flying swings."

"Oh, the swings got you, too, eh? I tried them with my nephew a couple years ago. I had the same experience," Matt said with a chuckle.

A customer walked in between them and turned to Matt. "You work here, right?"

Matt nodded. "I do. What can I help you with?"

"Well, my son wants a surfboard. We don't know where to start."

"Give me one minute, and I'll be right over to help you out," Matt said as he glanced at Lauren.

"I'll let you go. It was great talking," Lauren said as she turned toward the exit.

"Wait..." Matt said as then hesitated.

"What's up?" Lauren asked, feeling confused.

"I need to discuss something with you. It's kind of important. Just not here..."

Just then, Josh, one of the employees, came running over to Matt. "We're having an issue with the credit card reader, and there's a line."

Matt turned to Lauren. "I have to go, but we'll discuss this soon," he said with slight concern in his eyes.

Lauren watched as he hurried off, then she headed back onto the boardwalk, where a million thoughts went through her head. They barely knew each other. How could he have something so pressing to tell her?

CHAPTER NINE

"Dad, I worked in restaurants during college. Give me some training on managing Chipper's. I'm going to take over your position for the next couple of weeks because you need a break," Lauren said as she grabbed two plates of eggs over easy with home fries and pork roll from the heat lamp and set them in front of two customers sitting at the counter.

"I don't know about that. I can't put all of that on you," Joe said as he refilled some customers' coffee cups.

Lauren sighed and leaned on the register. "Just let me try to handle it. If it's too much, I'll let you know."

Joe hemmed and hawed. "I guess you're right. Plus, who knows when or if this sale will go through with Tony. I'm guessing probably after the summer is over. Seems like there's a lot of paperwork and logistics involved."

Lauren nodded. "We need to get you stress-free and healthy. Restaurants are too fast paced and chaotic for a retiree."

"Can you not call me a retiree? It makes me feel old," Joe said as he watched the host seat some people that had just walked in.

Lauren sighed, knowing full well her dad had a complex about getting older. Perhaps that was why he'd taken on Chipper's in the first place. Deep down, he probably didn't want to be retired.

A few tables paid and left, and it seemed things were quieting down for a moment, so Joe grabbed a notepad and pen and motioned for Lauren to follow him to the kitchen. "Now, Tuesdays is when the food delivery gets here. There's a binder in the back office that details everything we order and in what quantity. We'll get to that later. I have the employees sign in on the computer when they arrive and sign out when they leave to keep track of hours. Paydays are every Friday…"

Lauren listened intently and wrote down notes on the notepad. It seemed her dad was indeed ready to hand over the major restaurant responsibilities to her, and she needed to learn as much as she could quickly.

* * *

By two thirty, Chippers had been cleaned and shut down for the day, and the Fourth of July festivities were just starting for Lauren. The rest of the family had already secured a spot on the beach that morning, so Lauren met them there.

"So glad you could join us!" Claire yelled out as Lauren schlepped her beach chair, bag, and umbrella through the hot sand and dropped it all in front of Claire, who was packing the kids' sand toys into a bag.

"I'm pretty sure there's heat blisters on my feet right now," Lauren said as she plopped into an empty chair. "Are you leaving? Why are you packing your stuff up?"

"Because everyone else just arrived," Claire said as she took down her umbrella.

"Who?" Lauren asked while scanning the beach.

"Aunt Darlene, Uncle Charles, Aunt Kathy, and Uncle

Henry plus a boat load of cousins and their kids just got here. Too many to name with our big extended family."

Lauren squinted her eyes to see. "Where are they?"

Claire pointed ahead. "Under those blue pop-up tents. I was just about to take our stuff over there. I wanted to use the bathroom back at the house first, so I'm the last one to get over there. Well, and you."

"Is Brian coming?" Lauren asked as she got up from the chair.

"He is eventually. He ran out to get some extra things for the barbecue back at Mom and Dad's later."

They both got up and moved all of their belongings under one of the tents, then Lauren greeted all of the extended family members as well as her parents.

Everyone had their chairs positioned in a big circle so they could all talk and see each other. Bridget and Evan and the younger kids were building sandcastles in the middle of everyone, and the teenagers were about ten feet away, lying out in the sun on towels with music playing in their headphones, seemingly too cool for the adults. The older adults were together, talking on one side, and the cousins on the other. Lauren and Claire squeezed their chairs in with the cousins while Bon Jovi played through someone's speakers.

Heather, their cousin, slid her chair closer to Lauren. "So, I hear you're renting a house here for the entire summer?"

"I am. Wild, isn't it? The house is kind of dumpy, but it's grown on me, I have to say."

Claire cut in. "She's got this super-cute surfer neighbor, though."

Heather's ears perked up. "Oh yeah? Tell me more."

Lauren nodded. "He's cute and all, but I'm pretty sure he's taken. Though when I ran into him last week, he told me he had something important to tell me."

"What? You didn't tell me about that," Claire said, confused.

Lauren laughed. "Well, I'm telling you now. I guess I was afraid you'd blurt something out to him about it, like you've done in the past."

Claire rolled her eyes. "Whatever. Anyway, how has it been a week and you haven't found out what he has to tell you? I'm baffled."

Lauren sighed. "He got pulled away at his shop right after he mentioned it to me. I figured I'd run into him, and he'd tell me then, but I haven't seen him, and I don't have his number."

Heather leaned forward, fully invested in the conversation. "Go knock on his door."

Lauren shook her head. "I can't do that. If it's that important, he'll find a way to tell me. I'm not going to chase after him. I'm sure it's probably something about my house. Maybe he knows something that I don't."

Claire bit her lip. "Want me to find out? I can stop in Jungle Surf the next time I take the kids on the boardwalk."

"Absolutely not. I would be mortified," Lauren said as she leaned back in her chair and put on her baseball cap.

Heather leaned closer to Lauren. "Not to change the topic, but how are you doing since the divorce?"

Lauren shrugged. "Okay, I guess... but enough about me. How are *you*?"

Heather took a sip of her cold drink. "We can get to me shortly. I'd like to hear how you're doing."

Lauren took a deep breath. "Well, some days are good, and some days are bad. On the good days, I barely think about my old life with him. Usually, those days are when I'm busy with work, too busy to think about anything else. Then there's the quiet nights alone where I sometimes lie awake in bed, thinking of every happy memory we had together. Those are the nights where I usually cry myself to sleep. It's funny... how you can still mourn someone or the idea of someone even after they've shredded your heart to pieces and upended your life," Lauren said as she looked off toward the ocean.

Claire and Heather nodded, not sure of what to say, when suddenly a dance song came on the speakers. Roy, Janelle, Kristen, and Emily, the outgoing cousins, stood up and started dancing on the beach. Heather joined them then extended her hands to Lauren and Claire. "Get out here with us."

Lauren and Claire looked at each other and shrugged then popped out of their seats to dance with the rest of the crazy cousins. Lauren looked around at the group, who were laughing and enjoying themselves, and felt herself frozen in time and happy in that moment. It wasn't every day the whole family could get together, and here they were. She needed to savor this. Who knew when it would happen again.

* * *

After a big family barbecue back at Nancy and Joe's, everyone was back sitting on the beach on blankets and in chairs, waiting for the fireworks. The kids all had glow-stick necklaces and bracelets in every color, and they waved their lit sparklers in the air as the beach started filling with more people. It was a perfect warm night for a fireworks show. Lauren sat back in her chair while everyone else conversed, closed her eyes for a minute, and sank her feet into the cool sand while the ocean waves crashed gently.

Bang! Bang! Pop!

Lauren opened her eyes to see it wasn't the show that had started, but a few people sitting near them had brought their own fireworks that they were setting off. It made the sky brightly lit with gorgeous colors, and it was quite mesmerizing to see it so up close. She squinted and saw that it was her neighbor Erin and John, her husband, and some friends that were setting them off. She immediately got up and headed over toward them.

"Erin?" Lauren asked with a smile.

"Lauren! Look at us on the same beach," Erin said as she hugged her.

"I love your fireworks. It's working as a nice opener for the show at nine," Lauren said with a smile.

Erin shook her head and glanced at John, who was getting ready to set another firework off. "I don't want anything to do with them. He insists on doing it every year. I tell him to leave it to the professionals. What does he do? He sets them off anyway. He's giving me chest pains," she said just as another firework went off.

Lauren laughed and shrugged. "Well, I guess you like what you like."

Erin smiled. "Are you doing anything after? We're all going out on the boat afterward. John is hoping we'll catch some more fireworks. Maybe even see some far-off ones in Sea Isle or Atlantic City from over here in Ocean City."

Lauren looked back at her family, huddled together on blankets, talking. "Well, I think our extended family is going back to their hotel afterward, so I'll probably be heading home. Maybe I'll come. I have to see how I feel," she said with a yawn.

Erin paused in thought. "I think you should come. We're going to head out right after we leave here. Try to make it, would ya?"

"I'll do my best," Lauren said with a smile as she said goodbye and headed back to her chair just as the fireworks show from the barge was starting. Deep down, though, she was exhausted after working at Chipper's and spending the day in the sun socializing and eating barbecue. She just wanted to pass out in her bed.

* * *

Around ten p.m., Lauren yawned as she put her key in the door and stumbled into her house. It had felt like the longest but most wonderful day, and she was ready to go to sleep. She walked upstairs to the bathroom to wash her face, but some voices coming from Erin's house distracted her. She opened the window and peered out to see John starting up the boat and their friends walking on board.

Lauren walked away from the window and looked into the mirror above the sink. "You need to just go over there. It will be memorable," she said to her reflection. "You're only here until Labor Day. Make the most of this summer in Ocean City."

Lauren turned the bathroom light out, put her shoes back on, and headed out the door to Erin and John's boat. She had talked herself into it.

John was just about to untie the boat from the dock when Lauren arrived.

Erin screeched when she saw her. "You came!"

Lauren nodded as she walked on board, noticing it was pretty dark, and she could barely make out who anyone was.

Erin pointed at a padded bench in the back of the boat. "Why don't you take a seat back there," she said with a smirk on her face.

Lauren squinted to get a better look, noticing mostly everyone was sitting near the front of the boat. Why had Erin wanted her in the back? As John started driving the boat away from the dock, Lauren found a seat across from someone she couldn't see very well. She smiled and nodded at them then turned to put her arm on the railing, letting the breeze blow her hair off her neck.

"Lauren?" a familiar voice asked.

Lauren turned to see that unknown person. He had a hat on, which he turned backwards as the wind picked up.

"Matt? Is that you?"

Matt laughed. "It is. I see you got suckered into coming on the boat too."

Lauren smiled then glanced at the front of the boat to see

Erin staring at them while grinning. Lauren turned back to Matt. "I was so exhausted after working at the restaurant and spending the day on the beach. I kind of had to drag myself over here. I figured I might as well make the most of the time I have in Ocean City."

Matt nodded. "So, you're just here for the summer?"

"That's the plan. I came to help out with Chipper's, my family's restaurant. Though now, it looks like they're probably going to sell it," Lauren said as she glanced at Matt. "By the way, what's the important thing you had to tell me?"

Matt took a deep breath. "Yeah, about that. I don't know if it's my place to say anything, so I kind of chickened out with that, but now that you're here, I think you should know," he said as he got up and moved next to Lauren on her bench. "I think we can hear each other better this way now that the boat is going faster."

Lauren felt goose bumps rise on her legs and arms. "Do tell."

Matt nodded. "I saw Tony drop you off at your house last week."

"Oh, you know him?" Lauren asked, surprised.

Matt nodded but then turned serious. "The whole island knows him."

"Interesting," Lauren said as she scratched her chin in thought. "Well, what about him?"

"I heard you say your family is looking to sell Chipper's. Is he the potential buyer?" Matt asked.

"Yes, why?"

Matt looked up at the sky. "Let me put it this way. If that restaurant means anything to you and your family, don't sell it to him. He's known for buying up properties, then he levels them to the ground and puts something brand new in."

Lauren stared at Matt in disbelief. "I asked him specifically if he was going to keep the restaurant the same. He basically said yes."

Matt shook his head. "That's part of his strategy. He lies. He bought the beloved deli a few blocks down, family run for many years. He tore it up and put in a boutique clothing store. I'm talking five-hundred-dollar bathing suits, one-thousand-dollar handbags. He thinks he's in New York. Don't get me started on the gorgeous older residential homes that he knocked down to put in duplexes and triplexes. He's an investor. That's what he does, but he's not ethical about it like the others."

"You're one-hundred-percent sure about this? I need to know because I have to tell my parents," Lauren said, feeling frustrated by everything Matt was saying.

"Well, did he bring up his sob story about how his parents' restaurant in Atlantic City caught fire?" Matt asked.

"Yes, he did," Lauren said as she stared at Matt, waiting to hear what he had to say next.

Matt rolled his eyes. "Figures. That's all a lie. It never happened. They had a restaurant in Florida. His parents never even lived at the Jersey Shore. That restaurant did exist and did catch fire, but it was owned by the Faltones. I went to high school with their daughters... so I know."

Lauren placed her head in her hands. "Thank you for telling me this. I just feel sad for my parents. They were really looking forward to selling the restaurant and enjoying their retirement."

Matt lightly put his hand on Lauren's shoulder. "If I can be of any help with all of this, let me know, but I'm sure the right buyer is out there. I just wanted to make sure you knew what kind of guy Tony was."

As the boat picked up speed, the air was getting chillier and chillier, and Lauren felt sick to her stomach from the news, but somehow, having Matt right next to her warmed her entire body.

Just then, some wake caused the boat to rock from side to

side, and Lauren fell onto Matt. He instantly put his arm around her.

"You okay?" He chuckled.

Lauren sat up and composed herself. "Sorry about that."

Before Matt could say anything, John pointed at the sky just as some fireworks went off right above them, painting the entire sky red.

CHAPTER TEN

"Mom and Dad, why aren't you picking up?" Lauren asked into her phone, feeling frustrated. She'd called each of them a couple of times, but there wasn't an answer, and it was urgent.

Lauren grabbed her car keys and headed out the door. She knew where they were. It was early Tuesday morning, and it was their ritual to walk over the Ninth Street Bridge and back.

Lauren parked on the street and started walking over the bridge to try to catch her parents. It seemed a lot of people had the same idea of walking on the bridge that morning as she passed joggers, walkers, and even some birders who had stopped to use their binoculars. Lauren kept moving, glancing at the cars going by on the right then turning to gaze at the bay on the left. By the time she was halfway over the bridge, she finally saw her Mom and Dad coming toward her from the opposite direction.

"What are you doing out here? You should have told us you were coming," Nancy said, her big floppy hat and sunglasses shielding her face.

Lauren pulled them aside to give room to everyone passing them. "You weren't answering your phones, and I have something I need to tell you."

A look of concern came over Joe's face. "We left our phones back at the house. Is everything okay? What could possibly be so important that you had to track us down on the bridge?"

Nancy stared at Lauren. "Is it health-related? Are you sick?"

Lauren sighed. "No, I'm fine."

Joe cut in. "Well, jeez. That's a relief. Do you need money?"

Lauren laughed then grew serious. "No. Look, that Tony guy that wants to buy the restaurant? He's a phony. He's a liar. He can't buy Chipper's. I'm telling you right now. I needed to let you two know before you signed off any kind of contract with him."

Joe cocked his head in confusion. "How do you know this?"

Lauren started walking back toward the car, and they talked along the way. "My neighbor Matt knows him. Apparently, most of Ocean City does. Every property he's bought here, he's leveled to the ground and made it into something else. Which, fine, if the original owners don't care, but we want to preserve Chipper's, right?"

"Absolutely," Nancy said.

Joe nodded. "That's correct, but he stated to us that he planned to keep Chipper's as is, aside from some small fixes."

Lauren rolled her eyes. "He told me the same. He also told me a made-up story about his parents' restaurant in Atlantic City. I don't trust him for a minute."

Joe rubbed his forehead. "Well, what are we going to do? Wait for another buyer to come along? I guess we could get a Realtor involved, but I imagine selling a business is different from selling a house. I don't know what the market is for something like Chipper's."

Nancy shook her head. "We have to do something. This restaurant is taking a huge toll on us. I've never seen your father so stressed out."

Lauren thought for a moment then stopped in her tracks just as they reached the bottom of the bridge. "Take the rest of the summer off. I'm going to fill in for dad with managing Chipper's."

Joe shifted his eyes. "You were only going to fill in for me for the next couple of weeks, and now you want to manage for the next two months?"

Lauren nodded. "Yes. I think I can do it. Trust me. If I find that I can't, you'll be the first to know. Just keep your phone on you so I can call with questions, because I will have them."

Nancy lowered her sunglasses. "But what about *your* stress? That can't be healthy for you either."

"It's a small restaurant. I think I can manage, and if I can hire a few more servers, I don't have to worry about tables being taken care of. I can focus on everything else that needs to be done," Lauren said as she approached her car.

"Joe, what about days off? You barely took a day off. Now, Lauren is going to work continuously for two months?" Nancy asked as she turned to him.

"I barely took a day off because I chose to be there. It was my first time running a restaurant, and I wanted to make sure everything went smoothly. However, George, one of the cooks, has been there a long time and he knows how the place is run. He's good at opening and closing and keeping track of the employees as well as dealing with any customer issues, and the same for Carlos. I didn't need to be there every day, and neither does Lauren. She just needs to be there when George and Carlos are off. They get paid extra for managing when that's part of their duties for the day, so they know what they're doing," Joe said confidently. "I just had issues with giving up that control."

Nancy and Lauren each breathed a sigh of relief. It seemed everyone was on board with Lauren managing, and it appeared that it would all fall into place somehow.

"So, what am I going to do about Tony now if he calls? Tell him we aren't interested?" Joe asked.

"Yes," Lauren said sternly.

Joe nodded. "So, you really believe this neighbor of yours… What's his name again?"

"Matt," Lauren said, nodding. "I do. He has no reason to make all this up, and I can tell he's a good guy."

Joe scratched his neck. "A good guy, eh? I like the sound of that."

Nancy shook her head and rolled her eyes. "Come on, Joe. Let's get to the car."

"I'll talk to you guys later. I'm headed to the restaurant," Lauren said as she unlocked her car door.

"Tell everyone I'll be in to say hi, but I'm not staying," Joe said with a wink.

* * *

Back at Chipper's, Lauren arrived to a calm restaurant. George had opened and was busy flipping pancakes on the griddle behind the counter.

"Good morning!" George yelled over to Lauren as he flipped his last pancake and plated it up with some tabs of butter.

"Morning, George! How's it going?" Lauren asked as she scanned the restaurant.

"Great, as usual, but something's going on over there," George said while motioning with his head to a back booth.

Lauren glanced over to see Mr. Young in a booth, looking solemn as he ate his eggs and stared out the window at nothing. She immediately walked over and sat in his booth across from him. "Hey, Mr. Young, I'm not used to seeing you in a booth. You're always at the counter."

Mr. Young smiled when he saw Lauren. "I know. I guess I just wanted to be by myself with my thoughts today."

"What's going on?" Lauren asked as she propped her head on her hands.

Mr. Young looked her dead in the eye. "I heard through the grapevine that your parents are selling the restaurant."

"Well... that's correct. They're looking for a buyer. My parents are retired, and running this restaurant has been too much for them."

Mr. Young looked down at his eggs. "It just really bummed me out, hearing that. I've been coming here a long time. It would just make me sad to see Chipper's become something else. I don't have a wife or kids. This place is my family," he said as he looked over at George and nodded at him.

"You don't have to worry about the restaurant becoming something else, at least not now. My parents are being selective about who can purchase it. They want someone who wants to keep Chipper's open. Also, I'm going to be around a lot more because I'm taking over my dad's duties," Lauren said with a smile as she got up slowly from the booth.

Mr. Young breathed a sigh of relief. "It was so great talking to you. I'm glad you're here."

In that moment, Lauren realized that Chipper's was much more than an eating establishment to many of the locals and customers. It was a safe and welcoming place full of friends, family, laughter, and memories.

* * *

That evening, Lauren sat in bed with her back propped up with pillows, reading her newest book. The soft glow of her lamp on the end table lit the words on the pages, and the air was filled by the soft hum of the air conditioner in the window. It had been a very hot and humid day, nearing ninety-five degrees, and it seemed like it was taking forever for the room to cool down.

Suddenly, light tapping noises could be heard all around

her. Then they got louder and louder until a crack of thunder out of nowhere caused Lauren to jump out of bed in a panic. She ran to the window and looked out to see hard rain coming down in sheets. There were already mini rivers flowing down the sides of the street toward the storm drains, and a flash of lightning lit up the sky off in the distance.

Lauren got back in bed and tried to read, but the wind picking up outside distracted her. She reread the same sentence three times before she shut her book and put it back on the end table. She looked at the clock: eleven p.m. Then that was when it happened. The electricity went out.

"Just perfect," Lauren said as she searched around in the dark for her phone. She found it and turned on the flashlight then put on her slippers and stepped out into the dark hallway. The house she'd gotten so comfortable with was now scarier than ever. She was alone in the dark with just a cell phone flashlight, and since the air conditioning had turned off, it was getting hotter by the minute.

Lauren walked carefully down the steps, hearing every step creak as more thunder boomed in the background and rain pounded the roof and ground. She got to the kitchen, where she opened a drawer and pulled out an old pack of matches with a cowboy on it, which had been left in the house.

"Hopefully, these work," Lauren said as she walked into the living room and struck the first match. A flame immediately appeared, so she lit some taper candles in brass holders and walked to the window and pulled aside the curtain to watch puddles forming in the street and yard.

After about five minutes, she maneuvered away from the window and plopped into the uncomfortable wicker chair, where she stared at the shadows on the ceiling from the flickering flames as she dabbed the sweat on her forehead with a paper towel. The rain was just making the air muggier and more unbearable. Then it grew quieter and quieter until it appeared that the rain and wind had died down considerably.

She grabbed the candles in their holders, opened the front door, and stepped onto the covered porch. Outside, it was much cooler than it was inside, and she was grateful to be out there. She set the candlesticks on a small table and sat in a chair with her feet up on the railing.

Lauren eyed the other houses on the street, noticing how everyone's else's electricity also appeared to be out—either that, or they turned off every light in their houses when they went to bed. The rain was now just a mist, and the wind had disappeared with the thunder and lightning. She'd closed her eyes for a minute when she heard a door close next door. She looked over to see Matt taking a seat on his porch with candles as well. He glanced over at her and smiled.

"I see you had the same idea. Your electricity went out too?" Matt yelled over.

Lauren nodded. "Yes, and it's too hot to sit in there. I might be camping out here until the electricity is back on."

"I hear ya," Matt said then paused. "Feel like hanging out on my porch instead?"

Lauren felt her stomach drop. She was still in her pajamas and slippers, and her hair was in a messy bun. She didn't exactly feel presentable. "I don't know…"

"That's okay. I understand. Maybe another time," Matt said sheepishly.

Lauren stood up. "You know what? I'm coming over," she said as she picked up her two candlesticks and walked them over.

"Take a seat," Matt said with a smile as he patted a chair next to him on the porch when Lauren approached.

Lauren put the candlesticks on a table and plopped down, immediately pulling her knees to her chest and taking her hair out of her bun. "I'm dressed for bed. Don't mind me."

Matt laughed. "You look great. Don't worry about it. So, you got woken out of a dead sleep too?"

Lauren shook her head. "No, I was just reading in bed, but

boy is that house creepy when the electricity is out during a storm."

"I can imagine. Figures this happens during a heat wave, right?" Matt asked as he looked out toward the street, seeing steam coming off the asphalt.

"It's crazy. Oh, by the way, thank you for telling me about Tony. I let my parents know right away. They won't be selling to him."

Matt nodded. "Glad I could help. I hope your parents can find a better buyer that suits the business."

Lauren looked down at the floor. "Me too. My dad is having health issues from the stress of Chipper's. I came here this summer to help them out, but I don't know what's going to happen after that."

"Are you from around here?" Matt asked.

"I grew up in South Jersey but moved to Vermont for college and never moved back until now," Lauren said as she hugged her knees tighter. "What about you?"

"Vermont, eh? That's interesting. I'm actually from Ocean City. Born and raised here but left for Boston on a baseball scholarship. Ended up playing for the triple-A league and then finally made it to the Major Leagues and got a career-ending injury during my second game," he said as he rotated his shoulder.

"That's devastating. I'm so sorry to hear that. Which Major League team was it?" Lauren asked.

"I appreciate it. It was very upsetting for a while, but I think I've made a nice life for myself since. I was a short-lived relief pitcher for the Phillies. What about you? What were you doing in Vermont all of those years?"

Lauren smiled. "Well, I work in events, doing weddings and corporate conferences. My team takes care of the lighting and sound mainly, but we work alongside the caterers and florists and the people who put up those huge tents outside, among many other vendors." Lauren said as she drifted off in thought.

"In the summers when it was slow, I freelanced as a stage manager for Major League Baseball. What a small world."

Matt nodded. "Small world, indeed. Did you like living in Vermont?"

"I loved it. We lived in Burlington and had the most adorable house and yard near Lake Champlain and some fabulous restaurants," Lauren said, catching herself accidentally inserting Steven into the conversation.

Matt scratched his chin. "Oh… sounds nice."

Lauren sighed. "I guess I should clarify. I lived with my then husband. We have been divorced for six months. We just sold the house, and it just so happened to work out that I could live here for the summer."

"I get it. I'm also divorced. High school sweethearts who thought we wanted to be together forever and learned we weren't meant to be," Matt said with a nod.

"I wish my divorce was that amicable. It was pretty rough for a while. We were happily married… until suddenly, we weren't." Lauren cleared her throat. "Anyway, are you seeing anyone now?"

Matt shook his head. "Nope… not that I know of," he said with a smile.

Lauren thought back to the time she'd seen him kiss a woman in his home. "Really? I thought you had a girlfriend for some reason."

Matt paused in thought. "What made you think that?"

Lauren watched the flame flicker on the candle. "I was walking by when I first moved in and happened to see—"

Matt cut in. "My sister-in-law. I'm pretty sure that's who you saw. My brother and his wife were staying here for the week about the time you moved in."

"That explains it," Lauren said as she started to yawn. "Looks like the electricity is back on," she said, pointing inside Matt's house, noticing the lamps were now lit up.

Matt cocked his head to the side. "Well, I guess it is. That's a bummer."

"Why?" Lauren asked, confused.

"Because I was really enjoying sitting and talking with you out here," Matt said as he leaned back in his chair.

Lauren tried to hide her next yawn, but it sneaked out. She was dead tired even if her adrenaline was pumping talking to Matt. "We'll just have to do this again, huh?" she said while standing up then blew her candles out.

Matt smiled. "We definitely will."

CHAPTER ELEVEN

"Lauren, just let your father try to fix it. He knows a thing or two," Nancy said as she stood next to her, watching Joe struggle with the huge window-unit air conditioner.

"Dad, can I help?" Lauren asked as she grabbed one side of the air conditioner that had been hoisted out of the window.

"Set it down on the floor. Right here is good," Joe said as they lowered it down together.

Nancy took a napkin out of her purse and dabbed the sweat on Joe's forehead as he took apart the air conditioner.

"This stopped working last week, you said?" Joe asked.

Lauren nodded. "Yes, when the electricity went out with that big storm. It hasn't worked since. It just blows out warm air."

Joe shook his head as he held up the filter. "It's caked with tons of dirt and dust in this filter. Go wipe it out and clean it for starters. Let it completely dry before you put it back in," he said, handing it to Lauren.

Five minutes later, Lauren was back. "How's it looking? Do you think it can be fixed?"

Joe nodded. "Help me get it back in the window." They

both lifted the air conditioner into the living room window, then Joe turned it on. Immediately, cold air came flowing out.

"You did it. You fixed it. How did you do it?" Lauren asked, astonished. "I was almost certain I'd have to find a new one."

Joe wiped his hands on a bandana in his pocket. "I just so happened to have a replacement part in my toolbox from when our AC unit kicked the bucket at the old house. Figured I'd bring it over just in case that was the issue, and turns out it was."

"I'm thoroughly impressed," Lauren said as she held her hands in front of the cold air blowing out.

"Well, I guess we'll be going. You heading over to Chipper's?" Joe asked as he and Nancy stepped out onto the front porch, followed by Lauren.

"I am. Carlos is leaving early, so I'll be closing today," she said as she watched her parents head to their car.

Just then, Frank Sinatra could be heard blaring down the street, getting louder and louder as Tony pulled his Mercedes-Benz in front of Lauren's house. He got out and pulled his sunglasses off. "Well, well, well. Looks like I got here at a good time," Tony said as he brushed something off his suit jacket and eyed Nancy and Joe about to get in their car.

Lauren shifted her eyes. "Tony, what are you doing here?"

Tony glanced at Lauren and scoffed. "I've come to discuss my purchasing Chipper's."

Joe shook his head. "Tony, we already discussed this. We're not selling it to you. It's just not a good match."

Lauren nodded in agreement with her dad.

"Not a good match? *Not a good match?*" Tony yelled. "Do you know who you're talking to?"

Nancy crossed her arms and stared Tony down. "What's that supposed to mean?"

"It means that we already verbally agreed on this sale, and

I will be getting my lawyer involved," Tony said with a smirk. "Good luck with that, as my attorney is really good at his job."

"Verbally agreed? No, we discussed it. We never said that we were definitely selling it to you," Joe said as he felt his blood start to boil.

Tony laughed obnoxiously. "Whatever you say."

Lauren was so angry and upset that she felt tears welling up in her eyes. She looked over to see Matt walking on the sidewalk toward them.

"Remember me?" Matt said as he towered his six-foot-five body over Tony.

Tony took a couple of steps back. "What do you want? This doesn't involve you."

Matt rubbed his chin and thought for a moment. He leaned into Tony's ear. "See... it does involve me. These are my friends, and when I hear someone threatening them, I don't take too kindly to it. Not to mention you're a fraud, and everyone knows it. Hasn't Ocean City banned you yet? We all know the lies you tell sellers about your 'parents'' restaurant in Atlantic City."

"You're out of your mind. You know that?" Tony asked as he took a couple more steps back toward his car.

Matt stepped toward him again. "You see, Tony, I know a lot about you. A lot more than I should. I'm friends with a lot of people in Ocean City and the surrounding towns. My sister runs one of the biggest real estate offices in the area. I have the power to get you, as an investor, blackballed. Why? Because you lie and bully your way into sales. That's why. In fact, I got video of the entire interaction you just had with my friends out here, and because it's the new iPhone, you're easily identifiable."

Tony took a couple more steps back as Matt kept walking closer to him. "Now, you can leave these people alone and drive your little Mercedes-Benz out of here... or you can stay, and I can make sure you never buy another investment property in Ocean City again. Which will it be?"

Tony glanced at Joe and Nancy, who were watching the exchange with widened eyes then at Lauren, who was staring at Matt with adoration. "I guess I'll be going, then," he said as he quickly hopped into his car and took off down the street.

Matt watched as the car drove out of sight, then he turned to Nancy and Joe. "You don't have to worry about him bothering you again... but if he does, you let me know."

Joe walked toward Matt with his hand extended, and Matt shook his hand. "So, you're the neighbor Lauren was telling us about. Thank you."

Matt glanced over at Lauren and smiled. "That's me. It's nothing. I'm just trying to look out for you all."

Lauren felt her heart tumbling inside her chest. What had she just witnessed? She felt like she was living the scene of a movie where the cute guy next door saved the day. She snapped out of her thoughts when she noticed everyone was now looking at her. "Mom... Dad... This is Matt."

Nancy sighed. "We definitely dodged a bullet there, but it looks like we made a new friend. I'm Nancy, and this is my husband, Joe. Thank you again," she said as she got into the passenger side of the car. "Joe, let's go. I'm ten minutes late for my hair appointment!"

Joe stood staring at Matt in awe. "We'll chat another day. I'd love to hear your thoughts on maybe where we can find a good potential buyer," he said then walked to the car. "Lauren, call us later." Joe got into the driver's side, and off they went down the street.

It was just Matt and Lauren standing on the sidewalk together now. He was so tall and muscular. No wonder Tony was intimidated.

"Thank you for what you did," Lauren said, looking up at Matt as he flipped his hat backward. "You didn't get video of that whole exchange, did you?"

Matt laughed. "No, but he doesn't need to know that. I kind of had to outplay him at his own game to get him off your backs. I'm pretty sure it worked."

"I hope so," Lauren said as she glanced at her watch. "Man, I've got to get going. I'm closing the restaurant today."

"What time will you be done?" Matt asked as he put his hands in his pockets, which made him even cuter.

"Probably around two thirty."

"Well, I'm off work today. Feel like walking the boards with me tonight?" Matt asked.

Lauren could feel herself blushing, but she tried to subdue her excitement to play it cool. "That sounds like fun. I'm down."

"Perfect. Stop over around eight."

* * *

Around eight o'clock that evening, they were driving to the boardwalk in Matt's Wrangler with the windows down. The air was warm, and Matt's vehicle smelled of a mixture of beach and cologne. Lauren felt like she was in high school again, driving with the cutest guy in the school.

"Man, there isn't anywhere to park," Lauren said as she noticed meter after meter was taken.

Matt smiled. "Oh, I already have a spot to park. My friend lives on Sixth Street and lets me park in his driveway when I need to," he said as he turned left onto Sixth.

Minutes later, they were parked and walking on the boards.

"Wow, it really is a beautiful night," he said while glancing out toward the ocean then looking back at Lauren. "I know it's late, but are you hungry at all?"

Lauren nodded. "Actually, yeah. I was running errands after work and didn't have a chance to eat."

"Same. How about some pizza?" Matt asked as he looked ahead at the big lit-up sign at Manco & Manco Pizza.

"I'm down for pizza any time," Lauren said as she felt her stomach rumble.

They sat at a table at Manco's and ordered an entire plain pie with two root beers to drink.

Lauren bit into her slice and threw her head back and closed her eyes as she chewed and swallowed. "I feel like I'm eighteen again. That's one of the last times I had this pizza. It's just so good."

"Eighteen? So you really haven't been back to Ocean City in that long?" Matt asked, astonished. "I guess I'm just surprised since you're from around here."

Lauren shrugged. "I went off to college, and that was that. I never came home to Gloucester County much. It kind of forced my family to visit me in Vermont, though," she said with a wink.

Matt took a sip of his soda. "So what do you think of Ocean City now?"

Lauren watched the workers behind the counter prepare the pizza dough then ladle sauce and cheese onto the pies before putting them into the oven, then she glanced at all of the happy families, friends, and couples all around them. She smiled at Matt. "I have to say I'm really falling in love with this shore town. There's so much nostalgia that I forgot about. It's like rediscovering a long-lost friend. Not only that, but I think being by the beach has brought new life into me. It's hard to explain."

Matt nodded his head and kept his eyes on Lauren. "Do you mind me asking how old you are?"

"I'm forty-three. You?"

Matt smiled. "Also forty-three."

"Really? Class of ninety-eight?" Lauren asked.

"Yes, that's it," Matt said as he smiled. "How funny is that?"

Lauren smirked. "So we would have been in the same class. Figures."

Matt laughed. "Are you ready to head back out? I've got a great place to take you for some nineties nostalgia."

"Lead the way," Lauren said as she got up and followed Matt to the boards.

The boardwalk was crowded, but it oddly felt like she and Matt were the only ones there. They passed a bunch of shops until they got to the Surf Mall, where a big crowd stood out front.

Matt grabbed Lauren's hand. "Follow me," he said then led her through the many people to the back of the store to Rockstar Headquarters, where old and new band posters and T-shirts lined the walls and ceiling. Racks of Grateful Dead, the Beatles, the Rolling Stones, and other band T-shirts sat near the register, and to the left was a section with vinyl records.

"You have to see this," he said, taking her to a dark back room by the vinyl section.

Lauren gasped when they walked in. It was a black-light room with neon glow-in-the-dark posters. "This is a blast from the past," Lauren said as she walked around the room, stopping to stare at a neon-colored poster with mushrooms on it.

Matt laughed. "I just love this time capsule in the Surf Mall. It hasn't changed much since I was a teen. It's a source of comfort for me in an ever-changing world."

"I get it. I really do," Lauren said as she walked out of the room. She flipped through some records, holding up *Magical Mystery Tour*. "I fell in love with the Beatles in high school."

"Same here," Matt said as he stood next to Lauren, flipping records alongside her.

"Oh yeah? Well, I discovered my parents' dusty turntable stereo in the basement. I set it up and found their records, and they had all of the Beatles' albums," Lauren said with a smile.

"This is crazy," Matt said as he stared at her. "I did the same exact thing. Took it out of the basement and all. I ended up buying a nicer turntable as an adult, and I still love to collect and play records."

"Me too," Lauren said as she turned to Matt, feeling like they were way more similar than she had ever predicted.

"What else do we have in common?" Matt asked, reading Lauren's mind.

Lauren laughed. "Way too much already."

Matt bit his lip. "Do you like baseball?"

"Love it," Lauren said without hesitation.

Matt took a deep breath. "How long did you say you're in Ocean City for?"

Lauren thought for moment. "Until Labor Day, but I have no idea where I'm going to be living. I don't have a place in Vermont anymore."

"Right," Matt said as he pulled a Van Morrison record out and studied it.

Lauren changed the subject. "Do your parents live here?"

Matt nodded. "They do. As well as my sister and her family. We all just love it here—Did you want to head back out to the boardwalk?"

"Sure," Lauren said, then they walked together out of the Surf Mall, their hands grazing against each other.

Even though the crowds had dispersed, Matt reached for Lauren's hand again, but she was oblivious as she turned to look at some sunglasses. She put a pair of red heart sunglasses on and turned to Matt with a goofy expression. "Can I pull these off?"

Matt stared adoringly at Lauren. "You could pull any of these sunglasses off."

Lauren blushed and put the sunglasses back and led the way to the boards. She wasn't sure what was happening, but something was. There was some type of connection between them that she'd never expected.

Matt pointed ahead. "Do you wanna—"

"Play Skee-Ball?" Lauren cut in.

"How did you know I was going to ask that?" Matt asked as he playfully nudged Lauren with his hip.

"I didn't," Lauren said as she nudged him back.

Their hands grazed again while they maneuvered around all of the people on the boardwalk, and it made every goose bump on her body rise. Suddenly, she felt light-headed but overcome with happiness. Steven and she had gotten along, but they were so different from each other. She'd never connected with someone like this, and they'd barely scratched the surface.

CHAPTER TWELVE

"There you two are," Lauren said as she lugged her chair onto the beach and plopped it down right next to her parents. "I guess you left your phones at home again."

Joe lowered his sunglasses as he listened to the Phillies game on his small radio. "Yes, and on purpose. I'm sick of people having access to me twenty-four, seven. I miss the old days of when you were out, you were out, and if someone called, you got back to them when you got home. Your mother agrees."

Nancy nodded. "We're making lots of changes during this retirement. For one, we want to be more present and less involved with our phones."

"So I see," Lauren said as she glanced at Claire and Brian standing by the water, watching Bridget and Evan swimming.

"Took the day off today?" Joe asked.

Lauren nodded. "Yes, George opened, and Carlos is closing. I stopped in before I came here to check on things. Everything is good. So we're set... but I did have something I wanted to discuss with you two."

Nancy glanced at Joe. "Oh, no... not this again. Is Tony back?"

Lauren laughed. "No, he's long gone. Pretty sure Matt took care of that."

Joe shook his head. "That guy is *something*. He'll get what's coming to him," he said as he pulled his Italian hoagie out of the cooler and unwrapped it.

Nancy applied her suntan oil to her arms and legs. "Well, what is it then? Did you finally need some money?"

Lauren laughed. "Who can't use some money? But seriously... I just wanted to let you guys know that I spoke with the Realtor that I used to rent my Ocean City house, and I'm signing a one-year lease starting after Labor Day."

Joe was midbite and just about dropped half the hoagie in the sand. "You are?"

Nancy stopped applying her suntan oil and lowered her sunglasses. "Wait. You're going to live in Ocean City for a year? Did I hear that right? In that dump of a house?"

Lauren shrugged. "After we cleaned it up, it ended up being not too shabby of a house. It has good bones. It just needs some better furniture, some painting, and the carpets ripped out, which the owner is taking care of. Apparently, there's hardwood floors underneath. I'll be taking my furniture and belongings out of storage and bringing it all down here in a moving truck."

Joe took another bite of his hoagie just as a seagull tried to swoop down and steal it from him.

Nancy shrieked. "Joe, I told you that you had to come over here under the umbrella to eat that. Look at the birds, up there stalking you," she said glancing at the sky.

Joe moved his chair under the umbrella then took a bite and swallowed. "I apologize that I'm eating during your big news, but I'm starving."

Nancy rolled her eyes. "He acts like I don't feed him. I cooked him up a full breakfast this morning with scrapple, eggs, and toast."

Joe shrugged. "I can't help that I'm hungry. Something about being on the beach, I guess."

Nancy sat up in her chair. "Well, back to you, dear. We are just surprised you want to live in Ocean City... for the next year. You seemed eager to get back to Vermont. Don't you have to go back to your job?"

Lauren shook her head. "I told my job that I'm purchasing my parents' restaurant."

This time, Joe did drop part of the hoagie in the sand. "You're purchasing Chipper's?"

"Yes, I want to own Chipper's. I've really enjoyed working there this summer, and I feel like I have the hang of things now. I also want to figure something out for the old store attached to it. I figured I should take this opportunity," Lauren said, feeling relief settling in her chest.

"Chipper's closes for the season in September. What will you do for work?" Nancy asked.

Lauren paused in thought. "Well, I have options. I could try to keep Chipper's open all year round like some other eating establishments around here, or I could find another job... locally."

Joe shook his head. "You're not purchasing Chipper's."

"What? Why?" Lauren asked while holding her hands up in shock.

"Because we didn't purchase it. We were given Chipper's through the family. It's always been handed down. It hasn't been purchased since your grandparents bought it. In that sense, we would hand it down to you," Joe said with a slight smile forming on his face.

Lauren thought for a moment. "But you'd miss out on the money you'd get from selling the place. Would handing it down to me make things not as financially beneficial for you two? I mean, think of all the things you could do with that money. Get a boat... travel the world... home renovations... put in a pool..."

Nancy waved her hand in the air. "We are doing just fine. We both have pensions and retirement. I guess I'm just concerned that you're going to realize that owning a restaurant is not your life plan. Wouldn't you rather be working events in Vermont like you have been doing?"

Lauren sighed and looked out toward the ocean, now seeing Claire and Brian swimming alongside the kids, looking happier than ever. "I like working events, and I probably will miss it... but I know if I go back to Vermont, I'll also miss being here. I think I've just realized how much growing I've done since I came here. That divorce turned my world upside down. I went into a depression, and life just didn't feel like it would ever get better, and now it has. I want to at least try to make it work here. I need to give it a shot. I won't forgive myself if I don't."

Joe took the last bite of his hoagie. "Well, consider the restaurant yours, then."

"You're being serious right now?" Lauren asked.

Nancy nodded. "Yes. We're just excited to have you living near us again—"

"And to wipe our hands clean of the restaurant," Joe chimed in.

Lauren laughed. "All right, so this is really happening, then."

"We'll get all of the paperwork together to make it official," Nancy said as she leaned back in her chair.

Joe shifted his eyes. "Does this have to do with that neighbor guy of yours? Matt?"

"No, this is something I've been thinking about since before he and I started hanging out."

"Oh, you two have been hanging out some more?" Joe asked, fully ready to hear all of the details.

"Your father likes him," Nancy cut in.

Joe nodded. "I do. He's a stand-up guy. Looking out for my

daughter and her parents. You don't see many of those anymore."

Nancy laughed then glanced at Joe. "Can I tell her?"

"Tell her what?" Joe asked.

"How you acted that day…"

"Go ahead," Joe said as he turned down the Phillies game.

"He would not stop talking about Matt after that encounter with Tony. I've never seen him more impressed with someone," Nancy said with a smile.

Joe started putting on some sunblock. "Already, I can tell he's better than that deadbeat ex-husband of yours. What was his name?"

Lauren laughed. "You know his name. Steven."

"Oh, that's right. I guess I was trying to forget it. If I ever see that guy again, my hands are going around his neck," Joe said as he curled his lip.

Nancy quickly changed the subject. "We are just so pleased to hear this news. Make sure to tell Claire when she comes in from the ocean."

Lauren smiled. "We're sisters. She already knows," she said as she stood up from her chair then folded it up.

"Where are you going? You just got here," Joe said.

Lauren winked. "I'm meeting someone."

Nancy leaned forward. "Oh? Is it Matt?"

Lauren started walking away. "I'll let you know later. Have fun," she said, looking over her shoulder.

* * *

"In all of my years in Ocean City, I've never been to Corson's Inlet," Lauren said as she and Matt walked down a wooded beach trail toward the water.

"Really? That's surprising, but in a way, it isn't. Not everyone knows about it, or they do and it's not their thing since it's far away from the boardwalk and the hoopla, but that's the beauty of it," Matt said, smiling at Lauren.

Matt was a lot more tanned and had dirty blond hair from the sun. His arms popped in the black T-shirt he was wearing, and of course, he had a backwards hat on—Lauren's weakness.

They finally got to the beach on the inlet side. There were tons of clam shells by the water's edge, and on their left were all of the trees and vegetation.

"You have to get here around low tide, or there's not much beach to walk on out here. I had a friend who got stuck out here during high tide. He had to climb up into the vegetation to escape it," Matt said chuckling.

"Really? Jeez, that's a little scary," Lauren said as she glanced at the boats that had docked in different spots on the inlet. "That looks fun. It's a nice, calm spot to dock hang out and relax, it seems."

"Oh, it's great. The next time my friend invites me out on his boat, you'll have to come," Matt said as he stopped and looked in her eyes.

"That sounds great."

"Perfect," Matt said as he took off his backpack then he pulled out two towels and laid them on the sand. "I was thinking we could sit and watch the world go by here."

Lauren took a seat on the towel and watched as some jet skiers whizzed past, then she looked over to see some men standing around talking while casting their rods into the water. It was such a different vibe from sitting by the ocean, but she loved it.

Matt turned around to look behind him, then his eyes widened with excitement. "There's tons of those little hermit crabs back there. They dig those little holes and run into them when they see someone. They're so fun to watch."

Lauren turned around to look, noticing hundreds of them scurrying along. "Wow, look at them. There's so many fascinating creatures here."

Matt stared at Lauren then smiled. "Off topic, but it seems we have a lot in common, but I still feel like there's so much more to learn about you."

Lauren nodded. "Agreed. Well, start with asking me a question."

Matt rubbed his hands together in thought, but not for long. "You mentioned you're newly divorced and that it was rough. Can I ask what happened?"

Lauren cleared her throat then looked off into the distance, trying to figure out the best way to tell *that* story. "Well, we were, or so I believed at the time, a very happy couple. We had been together since college and married for twelve years. One day last August, we had this wonderful day together. We set up some raised beds to plant some vegetables in and joked around and laughed the entire time. Then he cooked us dinner on the grill, and the two of us had this perfect meal outside at the table in our beautiful yard. Then I left for a work trip the next day. I was gone for a week in Arizona, working a huge event for my company. Nothing seemed out of the ordinary. So I get home after a week, and Steven, my husband, seems a little distant. It bothered me, but I thought maybe he was just stressed about work. Then, a few days later, he was at work, and I was at home. It was a Wednesday morning. I remember it like it was yesterday. I was outside, weeding, and my neighbor Sue appeared next to me. I remember seeing her and feeling startled because I had no idea she was there—Anyway, she seemed nervous. I could tell something was wrong. Then she tells me that she had been conflicted for days about whether to say anything, but when she saw me outside, she decided she would. She and her husband saw Steven bring two separate women over to the house while I was gone."

Matt shook his head. "I'm so sorry."

Lauren shook her head also. "Well, Sue and her husband knew immediately that something was going on by the way his hand was on the small of their backs when they walked into the house together. They also caught him kissing one of the women in the doorway right before she left. They immediately knew he was cheating but weren't sure if maybe we had broken up and I had moved out at first. So I nearly threw up when Sue was telling me this. I had never felt my stomach sink like that. It was like everything started spinning, and I was now living in this alternate reality."

Matt put his hand on Lauren's hand. "I can't imagine the pain that caused."

"I think that's why it hurt so much. It had felt like we were more in love than ever. I was at my happiest. He appeared at his happiest. There weren't any signs that our marriage was going south. It just came out of the blue and took my legs out from underneath me. Eventually, I snooped around in his drawers and found some more clues that he had been cheating, before I confronted him. Initially, he denied it. Then when I mentioned what our neighbor told me, he came out with it." Lauren took a deep breath, feeling like she'd finally gotten what had been weighing her down for months off her chest.

Matt squeezed Lauren's hand and looked into her eyes. "If you ever need to talk about it, I'm here."

"Thank you," Lauren said as her heart perked up. "What's your divorce story?"

Matt sighed. "It's really boring, which I guess is a good thing. She and I were too different. She was big into the party scene, even into her late thirties. She'd sometimes stay out till four, five, six a.m. with friends then get up a few hours later for work the next day. She'd wake me up in the process of coming home too. It was a bit of a nightmare. I still don't know how she functioned the next day. It was fun in our twenties and maybe a little in our early thirties, but after that, it wasn't my thing any longer. I wanted to focus more on the simple ways of life, like grilling in the backyard and gardening, maybe some birdwatching here or there," he said, smiling at Lauren.

Lauren smiled back. "Sounds like my kind of day."

Matt intertwined his fingers in Lauren's. "Anyway, we mutually decided to divorce. That was three years ago, now. I moved back to Ocean City right after, bought this house, and started my business. I've dated off and on, but nothing has stuck. It's harder in your forties, but maybe not so much anymore."

Lauren blushed. "I guess now is a good time to tell you that I just signed a year-long lease for my rental starting in September. I'm going to be the new owner of Chipper's."

Matt laughed and clapped his hands. "Well, that's an amazing turn of events. Even better than getting Tony out of there. Congratulations!"

"Thank you. I appreciate it," Lauren said as some people walked by.

"I'm really glad to hear you're staying," Matt said with a smile.

Lauren blushed. "The owner is fixing the house up a little for me too… and I'll be renting a moving van to bring my stuff out of storage in Vermont. I plan to make the house even nicer for my stay," Lauren said as she looked back to see the hermit crabs starting to encroach on their towels. "Maybe we should get out of their way." She pointed.

Matt glanced back then immediately stood up. "Yep, time to move. There is a neighborhood block party going on that we should attend, though. Have you heard of it?"

Lauren shook her head. "I don't think so. Erin might have said something to me about it in passing, but I don't remember."

Matt smiled. "You're going to love it. We do it every year. Let's head over that way now," he said, looking at his watch.

* * *

They arrived back at their houses to find a closed-off street. One of the neighbors was playing songs with his band on his front lawn, and another neighbor was cooking crabs outside in a big pot on a portable gas stove. Erin had a table set up with a minibar full of beer and wine plus sodas and waters, and another neighbor had a whole slew of games set up, like cornhole and ladder ball, which both the kids and the adults loved. Farther down the street was a bounce house someone had rented and even more tables of food.

They walked down the street, saying hi to different neighbors. Matt introduced Lauren to a few she hadn't met yet. Everyone they passed smiled and nodded.

"Why do I feel like they're staring at us?" Lauren asked under her breath as they continued walking through the street.

Matt chuckled. "I'm kind of getting that too. I don't think they're used to seeing me with someone. Maybe they're trying to figure out what we are."

Lauren felt her heart flip just as Erin approached them. "There you two are! We were wondering if you were coming. Care to come sit and have drinks with us over there?" she asked, pointing toward a big group of people sitting in the street in front of her house.

Matt shrugged and glanced at Lauren. "Sure, why not?"

They stopped at Matt's house and grabbed two folding chairs from the porch, picked up two bottles of beer from the table, and plopped down with the group.

"This is Lauren, everybody!" Erin yelled out.

"Oh… you're the one renting that old house. We've seen you coming and going. How do you like it? By the way, I'm Debbie. I live across the street from you, but our paths never seem to cross."

Matt nudged Lauren. "I had the same issue for a while."

Lauren smirked at Matt then glanced at Debbie. "I honestly love it. It needs some work, but it's such a great location and neighborhood. Plus, I'll be around for at least another year. I'm taking over my family's business, Chipper's."

"Chipper's? We love it there," Debbie's husband, Todd, cut in.

"Glad to hear that. It really is a great place."

Everyone else in the large group started talking to each other, and it grew quite loud. Matt and Lauren inched their chairs closer together, watching the band play while relaxing.

Matt turned to her. "I saw you that day you moved in."

Lauren's ears perked up. "Oh? Did you see when I hid on the porch behind my sister?"

Matt laughed. "I did. I thought it was adorable... and from what I saw of you, found you to be gorgeous."

Lauren turned red from embarrassment. "Thank you, but I was hoping you didn't see that. Also, I told my sister that you looked like a Calvin Klein model."

Matt chuckled. "I don't know if that's a compliment or not."

Lauren nodded. "Oh, it's definitely a compliment."

Matt leaned in toward Lauren and gently put his hand on her chin then gave her a kiss.

Lauren felt like melting away into her seat. How had a summer at forty-three given her the best summer romance of her life? She sat back in her chair just as Matt grabbed her hand and held it. Then, she looked around at all of the happy neighbors, smelled the bay air, and watched some seagulls pass overhead. She was smitten with Matt, but she was also completely smitten with Ocean City.

EPILOGUE

It was mid-August, and Lauren was at Chipper's, delivering some of their hot iced cinnamon rolls to a table, when she felt her phone vibrating in her pocket. She stepped outside near the back of the restaurant to take the call.

"Hello?"

"Hi, is this... Lauren?" an older gentleman asked.

"This is she."

The man cleared his throat. "This is Fred. I own the house on Bay Road that I believe you're currently renting. Jen, the Realtor gave me your number."

"Oh, hi, Fred. Nice to finally talk to you. I've really grown to love the house," Lauren said as she looked toward the beach, noticing what a beautiful sunny day it was.

"That's great to hear. I know you signed a one-year lease. Jen said that you're staying to take over your family's business, Chipper's. Is that right?"

"That is correct. I'm newly divorced, and my parents are too stressed out to handle the business during retirement. So, I'm happy to give it a shot."

"Well, I was wondering if you'd be interested in purchasing the property instead of renting," Fred said.

Lauren shook her head. "Fred, this property, even with all of the work it needs, would be way out of my budget. The location alone could get you at least a million. I don't have that kind of money."

Fred laughed. "I don't need a million. I have more than enough money to get by. Trust me."

Lauren was confused. She could have sworn Jen mentioned that Fred *needed* the rental money for his new place.

"The reason I'm asking if you'd like to buy the place is because I'd like it to go to someone who wants to fix it up and make it a beautiful home without taking away the old charm," Fred said, nodding. "I moved to Florida years ago and haven't been back. My old friend Herb lived in that house until he passed. He left the house to me. It was his childhood home, and I know that house and neighborhood meant a lot to him."

Lauren held her hand to her mouth. "Fred, we just went through the same scenario with Chipper's. An investor wanted to buy it, and I found out that he wanted to tear it down and put something else up. It's sort of why I decided to take it over."

"I know. I heard through the grapevine. It's why I think you'd be the perfect buyer. I would give you a really good deal on the house. Like I said, I don't need the money. I think we should talk and come to a price that works for both of us," Fred said.

Lauren took a deep breath. Everything was hitting so fast all of a sudden, and she needed life to slow down for a just a minute, but this was a huge opportunity.

* * *

Pick up **Book 2** in the Ocean City Tides series**, Ocean City Sunglow,** to follow Lauren, Matt, and the rest of the bunch.

. . .

Have you read the Cape May Series? If not, start with book 1, **The Cape May Garden**.

ABOUT THE AUTHOR

Claudia Vance is a writer of women's fiction and clean romance. She writes feel good reads that take you to places you'd like to visit with characters you'd want to get to know.

She lives with her boyfriend and two cats in a charming small town in New Jersey, not too far from the beautiful beach town of Cape May. She worked behind the scenes on television shows and film sets for many years, and she's an avid gardener and nature lover.

Printed in the USA
CPSIA information can be obtained
at www.ICGtesting.com
CBHW020819170724
11649CB00046B/437

9 781956 320145